D1738069

THIS DELUXE SIGNED EDITION OF

CAMP PLEASANT

Richard Matheson

IS LIMITED TO 1000 SIGNED COPIES

This is Number 949

CAMP PLEASANT

Camp Pleasant

Richard Matheson

CEMETERY DANCE PUBLICATIONS

G&G BOOKS

Baltimore
❖ 2001 ❖

Cemetery Dance Publications/G&G Books Edition 2001
ISBN 1-58767-014-3

24866005 8/01

All persons in this book are fictitious, and any resemblance that may seem to exist to actual persons living or dead is purely coincidental. This is a work of fiction.

Dust Jacket Art: © 2001 by Harry O. Morris
Dust Jacket Design: Gail Cross
Typesetting and Design: Bill Walker
Printed in the United States of America

Cemetery Dance Publications
P.O. Box 943
Abingdon, MD 21009
http://www.cemeterydance.com

G&G Book
3601 Skylark Lane SE
Cedar Rapids, IA 52403

FIRST EDITION

10 9 8 7 6 5 4 3 2 1

To my father,
Scarcely known
but always remembered

ONE

1.

The train wheezed into Emmetsville at nine-sixteen that Saturday night.

"You win." Bob handed me a dime. "I thought we'd have to get out and push."

Bob and Mack and I dragged our suitcases off the overhead racks and lugged them down the aisle. "Emmetsville! End of the line!" the conductor's voice came drifting down from the next car. "You're telling me," Bob muttered.

Our shoes crunched across the gravel as we headed for the station waiting room. It was getting chilly out and I could feel the night air through the thinness of my jacket.

"Listen to that engine," Bob said. "Sounds like an old lady after a hundred yard dash. I'm surprised we ever got here."

"We're here, ain't we?" Mack said.

"Yowza," Bob said. "Yowza, Mack boy."

The waiting room was small and smelled of rotting wood and disinfectant. Bob and I put down our luggage and stood waiting while Mack went over to the ticket window and asked the man how we got to Camp Pleasant.

"There's no bus," he said when he came back.

"What about taxis?" I asked.

"No taxis either."

"Fine," Bob said. "What do we do—walk?"

Mack gave him a withering look. "You can walk if you wanna," he said, "I'm ridin'."

"What are you gonna ride, your suitcase?" Bob asked.

"Wait and see, jerk," Mack answered.

We picked up our luggage and followed him out onto the street. He turned left and started walking along the sidewalk as if he wasn't carrying two heavy suitcases.

"What's muscle-head up to now?" Bob wondered.

"Wait and see, jerk," I imitated Mack's guttural voice.

Halfway down the block there was a drugstore which Mack went into. We followed him and put down our luggage again. Mack was thumbing slowly through the telephone book as we walked over to him.

"Who you gonna call, the Red Cross?" Bob asked.

"Stop shootin' off your mouth and you'll see," Mack said.

He didn't find what he was looking for though and a confused look crossed his face.

"Are you trying to find the camp's number?" I asked him.

"Yeah, but it's not here."

"The camp's probably in another county," I said. "Why don't you call information?"

"That's right," Mack said, nodding. He glanced at Bob. "Why don't you use your brains like Matt?"

"I yust come over on the ferryboat," Bob told him.

"The *fairy*boat," Mack said, reaching into his pocket for change.

Bob and I went over to the fountain for coffee while we waited.

"That guy kills me," Bob said. "If you go in for anything besides sports and screwing, Mack thinks you're queer."

I shrugged. "Don't let it bother you," I said.

"Yowza," Bob said and the girl brought us our coffee.

2.

The truck groaned to a halt in front of the drugstore and a short, well-built man, about thirty, got out of the cab. He was wearing blue denims and had a tan corduroy jacket over his sweat shirt. There were sneakers on his feet, a dark baseball cap on his head.

"Hi, fellas," he said, sticking out his hand. "I'm Sid Goldberg, head of the Senior Division."

We shook hands.

"You're in my division, Harper," he told me. "Cabin thirteen."

I nodded and smiled. "Swell."

We put our luggage on the back of the truck and Mack got into the cab.

"Good old Mack," Bob said as we climbed up on the truck. "Always in there."

"We'd better sit behind the cab," I said. "It's liable to be a little windy." We sat down on our upright suitcases.

"All set?" Sid Goldberg called and we called back that we were.

The motor coughed into life and we felt that truck jolt under us as it picked up speed. Immediately, a cold wind rushed down over us, ruffling our hair, penetrating our jackets.

"What makes you think it's going to be windy?" Bob asked, his face lost behind wind-flying hair.

"Just a suspicion," I answered.

We had to bend over at the waist to keep the direct blast off our heads. We crossed our arms and tried to keep warm, at the same time trying to keep the suitcases steady.

"This is the life!" Bob said. "A leisurely summer in the country!"

Sid Goldberg kept driving faster and faster. By the time we were out of town, the truck was doing seventy, roaring and rocking along the dark country road. Bob and I kept losing balance and falling against each other.

"*Jesus!*" Bob shouted. "This guy must have learned to drive on the Indianapolis Speedway!"

His suitcase fell over suddenly and he went flopping on the floor of the truck. Over the whistling rush of wind I heard his cursing and watched him lunge at his suitcase which was sliding away from him.

"What a way to start the summer!" he shouted when he was back beside me but I couldn't answer because I was laughing too hard.

"That's right, laugh, you bastard!" he screamed. "I could've broken my neck!"

In a minute, freezing, rocking, blinded by blowing hair, he was laughing as hard as I was.

3.

The truck rolled down the pebble-strewn path into Camp Pleasant, low-hanging branches brushing and scraping across the cab roof and swishing over our heads.

"There," I said, "that wasn't so bad, was it?"

"I hope the dispensary's open," Bob answered. "My can is fractured."

Sid Goldberg braked the truck in front of a large, dark building.

"The dining hall," Bob muttered as we both stood. We handed the luggage to Sid Goldberg and Mack, then jumped down onto the ground.

"Ooh, my legs," Bob said.

"S'matter, boys, have a rough ride?" Mack asked blandly.

"You bastard," Bob muttered.

"All right, fellas," Sid told us. "You wanna follow me? I'll show you where to bunk down tonight."

We trudged behind him under the high darkness toward a dark building on the shore of the lake.

"This is where we put on most of our shows," Bob told me as we scuffed down the path. "They show movies here on Wednesday nights and have song fests."

I grunted acknowledgment. The song fests would be my job. I was to be the music director; the first the camp had ever had.

We reached the lodge and Sid pushed open the door. It was pitch black inside, smelling of damp wood and molding mattresses. Our footsteps echoed off the high ceiling as we walked across the floor.

"Take your choice," Sid said, his voice sounding hollow. "One's about as good as another."

Back in the cabin, Sid waited until Mack got the battery lamp from his suitcase and set it on one of the upper bunks. Then he said, "I think you're all squared away now. You can let down the window shutters if you want more air. And you know where Paradise is."

"Yeah," Mack said. This was his third year at Camp Pleasant. He worked on the waterfront.

"Glad to have met you fellas," Sid said. "I'll see you in the morning."

He left us and became a thin beam of light dwindling off into the darkness. Bob and I got pajamas from our suitcases while Mack stripped off his clothes and put a striped bathrobe over his thickly muscled body.

"What's Paradise?" I asked.

"The head," Mack said. "Where I'm going now to drop one."

"How delicate," Bob said.

Mack snorted. "Oh, ex-*cuse me*! I mean—I am going to have a *bowel* movement."

When Mack was gone, I propped my flashlight on the bunk I'd picked.

"Doesn't he like you?" I asked.

"Oh, muscle-head's all right," Bob said. "He's an oaf, that's all." He slipped on his terrycloth bathrobe. "When he gets to know you better, he'll start on you too."

The walk to Paradise was a long one over rough ground, under the rustle of four-story pine trees, between rows of dark cabins, set to the music of crickets and the occasional, far-off belch of a frog.

"The Senior Division is the farthest one from Paradise," Bob told me as we walked. "Then the Intermediate, then the Junior. I guess they figure the younger they are, the harder it is for them to hold it."

"You have a Junior cabin, don't you?"

"Good God, no, Intermediate. I wouldn't take a Junior cabin on a bet. You always get stuck with a couple of sailors."

"What's that?"

"Kid who wets his bed at night. Boy, can they stink up a cabin."

Paradise was a tall building on the edge of the woods, built like the others, with logs and rough planking. We went up the long flight of steps and through the front doorway. As we entered, Mack was standing on one side of the long double row of sinks that ended in a small shower room. As he brushed his teeth, the buttery glow of his lamp lit his broad hair-swirled chest. I joined him at the sinks while Bob went into the other section where the toilets were.

I washed my hands and face, then took the toothbrush from my toilet case and pressed a half inch of paste onto the bristles. In the other room, Bob was singing soulfully — *"I'm a little teapot short and stout. Here is my handle, here is my spout."*

"What do ya think of this guy, Goldberg?" Mack asked me.

"I don't know," I said. "Was he here last year?"

"No. We had Johnny Wilson but he's in the Marines now. He was a good joe."

I nodded. "Goldberg's probably all right too."

"We'll wait and see," Mack said. "You can't ever tell about these kikes."

Later, while we were making our beds, I asked Bob why we were in camp three days before the kids arrived.

"Man, you have to *earn* your hundred and fifty when you work for Big Ed," Bob told me. "We'll be cutting grass and sweeping floors and lugging mattresses and trunks and every damn thing the next three days."

"Well, isn't that *too* bad," Mack said, zipping his nude body up in his sleeping bag. "You'll get those lily-white hands all dirty."

"Screw you," Bob said.

"You'd like to," Mack answered.

"No," said Bob. "As a matter of fact, dear boy, the very concept repels me."

"Well, *good night*, dear boy!" Mack threw back in a labored falsetto and turned on his bulky side, muttering to himself, "Another goddam Merv."

"Yowza," Bob said tiredly. I wondered who Merv was.

We got into our bunks and Bob lit a cigarette before going to sleep.

"Yeah," he said to me, "You've got quite an experience ahead of you meeting Big Ed Nolan."

"Yeah, he don't like you either," contributed Mack.

"His scorn is my badge of honor," Bob answered.

"Aah, shut up," Mack growled. "Someone wants to sleep."

"Someone?" Bob said, his voice suddenly dramatic. "Who can this someone be? Laocoon? King Henry the Fifth? Saint Augustine? Little Nemo?"

"Shit," Mack said.

"Ah," Bob said, "it is he, Mack Muscle-Head."

"You want *your* head handed to ya?" Mack asked.

"No," Bob sotto voced, "I need it. I own a hat. Good night, all."

4.

The bugle blew me out of Julia's arms and, for one hideous moment, I thought I was back in that country hospital again, screaming as the doctors, telling them she wasn't dead and I'd kill them if they touched her.

Then I looked out the screen door and saw the mist-covered lake and heard the bright singing of birds. There was a thumping sound and, looking toward the bunks on the opposite wall, I saw Mack reaching for his underwear. I got up and pulled off the top of my pajamas.

"Up," I said to Bob, "and at them."

"Forward my remains to mother," his muffled voice came filtering through the blankets.

"How soon is breakfast?" I asked Mack.

"Half hour after reveille," he said. I nodded, then looked over again at the comatose mound that was Bob Dalrymple.

"Come on," I told him.

Bob drew back the covers from his sleep-numbed features. "Behold," he said, "the face of death."

"Okay, jerk!" Mack said loudly, "hit the deck!" He grabbed the bedclothes and dragged Bob off the edge of the bunk. Bob hit the deck on three points, his outraged curse bounding off the cabin walls. Mack grabbed his toilet kit and left while Bob half-sat, half-lay on the floor, looking dizzy.

"Ain't he sweet?" he said.

"Get dressed," I told him.

Twenty minutes later, we were approaching the front of the dining hall where a cluster of men stood, two of them middle-aged, the rest in their early twenties. I recognized "Doc" Rainey, the assistant camp director who had hired me in the city; but the rest of the group, except for Mack and Sid Goldberg, were strangers.

"Nolan here?" I asked Bob as we crossed the log bridge.

"Uh-uh. He's probably in the kitchen stuffing his gut with bacon."

"You really go for him, don't you?" I said.

"Wait," was all he answered.

We reached the group and Doc shook my hand, then introduced me to the others. There was Jack Stauffer, the bulky water-front director, old Barney Wright who headed field athletics, Mick Curleman who ran the craft shop; plus an assortment of cabin counselors, each of whom worked on the waterfront, the athletic fields or the craft shop.

While we were standing there, a tall bony man in his early thirties came walking around the edge of the dining hall and joined us. He was wearing a tee-shirt and very abbreviated shorts which revealed two long, skinny legs ending in tennis shoes.

"Matt, this is Merv Loomis," Bob introduced him. "He's in charge of hikes."

"I'm delighted," he said when Bob told me I was going to be the music director. "Culture in this camp, with all due respect to the efforts

15

of our esteemed dramatics director—" he bowed to Bob—"has, in the past, been largely confined to horseshoes and butterfly mounting."

It was easy to see why Mack thought what he did about Merv—Merv with his gaunt, patrician face, his close brush cut, his immaculate use of words. I liked him though.

"I'm afraid you'll find your job fast assuming the proportions of an epic venture," Merv said when I told him of my hopes of forming the glee club among the boys. "The little reptiles would sooner cut their throats than sing a song."

The door was opened then by one of the kitchen help and we filed into the dim coolness of the dining hall.

There was a young woman sitting at the large table. She smiled at all of us as we approached, our footsteps echoing in the great room. I heard some of the counselors call her Ellen and Doc Rainey said, "Good morning, my dear," to her.

"Who's she?" I whispered to Merv as he sat down between Bob and myself.

"Ellen Nolan," he said.

"His daughter?"

"No, dear boy," Merv said, amusedly, "his wife."

I confess to a frank staring at her. Since I'd first heard of Ed Nolan, I'd thought of him as a middle-aged man. Certainly, Bob's descriptions of him had done nothing to alter that idea.

Ellen Nolan couldn't have been a day over twenty-one, I thought. She was a frail-looking woman, a little pale, her eyes brown and very large. Thick, auburn hair fell to her shoulders, drawn and ribboned behind her small ears. Her lips, as she smiled, were thin and had no lipstick. She was wearing a cotton dress, white with green squares on it and, from what I could see of her figure, it was as slight and fragile as her face. She was almost an opposite to Julia, the thought occurred painfully. Julia, tall, blonde, Amazonian.

I tried not to think about her but I couldn't help it.

We were breaking open our cereal boxes when Bob said, "Here comes Big Ed."

I looked up, curious, to see that my original conception of Ed Nolan was quite accurate. He was middle-aged, semi-bald, a great hulk of a man squeaking over the floorboards like an ape in sneakers, his face broad and red-flushed behind rimless glasses, the contour of his thick-lipped mouth broken by the dark jutting of an unlit, half-smoked cigar.

A general murmur of "Hi ya, Ed," went up from the counselors and he raised one paw of a hand in greeting, not the remotest flicker of change on his face. He sank down heavily in the chair beside his wife's and I saw her wince as he, quite obviously, pinched her under the table. He plucked the cigar from his mouth, laid it beside his plate, quaffed down orange juice in a swallow and refilled his glass to the brim.

"Ed is hungry," Bob murmured beneath the general chatter of conversation at the table. "He's probably had ten or eleven rashers of bacon and a few dozen eggs."

While we ate I looked over at Nolan. He was wolfing down cereal, his cheeks bulging with spoonfuls of it, heavily sugared. I noticed the small hole in his tee-shirt through which protruded tufts of black hair. Directly under his large pectorals began the downward bulge of his belly. I glanced at his wife. She seemed so out of place next to Nolan; like a fawn coupled to a grizzly bear. Once, she looked up before I could glance away and, for an instant, I unable to take my eyes from hers. She smiled a little at me and I felt a shudder run down my back as I reached for the newly brought plate of scrambled eggs.

In the middle of eggs and toast Nolan rose and stood silently until the noise had abated and the eating ceased. Then he picked the cigar from his mouth and spoke.

"Some of you have been with me before," he said. "Some of you are here for the first time. But remember this—all of you. No matter if you're new here or you know the ropes—I expect good work from you. You're being paid for it and that's the way I want my camp run."

While Ed Nolan talked, I looked at his wife. She was staring at the table and there was a look of strange, bleak emptiness in her eyes.

5.

Directly after breakfast, Bob and I retired to the fields to scythe until the ground was thick with mown grass, the air heavy with the hot smell of sap and pollen dust. We worked under an over blast of sunlight, the salty taste of sweat in our mouths. I hadn't done manual labor since the army and that morning did me in. By ten I had to handkerchief my right hand to protect the blisters. By eleven I was starting to burn and had to put my tee-shirt back on; by twelve the burning ache had penetrated to my muscles. I sat stiff and miserable at lunch, downing nevertheless, a gigantic meal.

Happily, lunch was followed by an hour's rest period, a regular feature of Camp Pleasant's schedule. I slept heavily and motionlessly on the cabin bunk until Bob shook me back to consciousness. Groggy with sleep, I trudged back to the fields again for an afternoon of gathering up the cut grass and stuffing it into sacks which we tossed on the truck so Sid Goldberg could drive them to the giant incinerator.

At four-thirty, Big Ed pronounced the lake open. I wanted to head for my bunk and sleep again but Bob managed to talk me out of it. I was glad he did. The lake was barely cool and it soothed my muscles to feel the water stroking them.

Supper was at five-thirty. Ellen Nolan wasn't there. When I asked Bob about it he said that there was a kitchen in the Nolan's cabin and, sometimes, Ellen Nolan ate there instead of going to the dining hall.

The meal was interrupted at mid-point by another Nolan speech. He told us that we had only three days to get the camp into "topnotch" shape and if we didn't "get into high gear" he'd have to take away our swimming time and cut the rest period in half. The camp, he said, had always been in "topnotch" shape on opening day and, by God, he was going to see to it that it was this year too.

When Big Ed had finished, we returned to our cold supper and finished it. Afterward, Bob, Merv and I took the half-mile walk up the road to the small grocery store. There, we sat on the porch, sipping Cokes, Merv smoking his slender pipe, Bob a cigarette.

"Does he always give speeches?" I asked.

"Incessantly," Bob said.

"How bad is he really?" I asked.

"He represents," Merv said, "all that is dismaying in the world. His insensibility to the feeling of others is shocking. His crushing approach to human relations is hideous."

"You make him sound like Hitler," I said.

"In his own oafish way," Merv said, "Ed Nolan has reduced Camp Pleasant to a microcosm of the Third Reich."

"Why do you stand for it?" I asked. "Why do the kids' parents stand for it?"

"To answer the first question," Merv answered, "Bob and I come here because we like the camp and the country. I worked in this camp years before Nolan came and I'm certainly not going to let him keep me from my summer here which I enjoy. As to opposing him, however, this is tantamount to an attempt to bash in the side of a tank with a daisy. Nolan has the support of the parents for the simple reason that they don't know about him. Kids don't talk about discipline unless it's fresh in their minds or done to crushing excess. Ed knows the limits. He always slacks off around visiting day and toward the end of each camping period."

"Then he's not dumb," I said.

"Oh no, he has great animal cunning," Merv conceded, "which is, precisely, what makes him so dangerous."

I put down my empty Coke bottle.

"Looks like I'm in for a grand summer," I said.

"Oh, don't worry about it," Bob said. "Just stay out of his way and he won't even notice you.

I tried to console myself with that.

6.

In the evenings, the Nolan's cabin was open house to Camp Pleasant personnel. There was a record player, current magazines, checker, chess and card games and a screened-in porch of wicker chairs where one could sit and gaze at the night-shrouded lake.

I wanted to go to bed but Bob talked me into a game of chess before sacking out. So, after returning from the grocery store, we started for the Nolan cabin, Merv leaving us with the statement that he had some reading to do.

"He doesn't ever go to Ed's cabin," Bob said. "There's a lot of tension between them. Ed hates him, I think. He's been trying to oust Merv for years but Merv is almost an institution in the camp and the only one who knows the surrounding country well enough to organize hikes." Bob shook his head. "Ed keeps looking for some excuse to get rid of Merv. Maybe some day he'll find one."

We walked along the trail past the wooden-floored tent where Sid Goldberg, Barney Wright and the heads of the Junior and Intermediate sections lived. Sid was sitting on the small porch, his legs propped up on the railing. He greeted us and we said hello as we passed.

"He seems like a nice fella," Bob said, "even if he is a dirty kike."

"Mack been at you too?" I asked.

"Yowza." Bob pointed to a little cabin in a patch of trees. "That's where Jack Stauffer and his wife live," he said. "Doc Rainey used to live there but he let Jack have it last year after Jack got married. Doc lives in a little tent by the water. He's a good guy, Doc. He should be head of the camp."

The trail turned left now and I saw, at its foot, a moderately sized log cabin with yellow curtains in the windows.

"There's Ellen Nolan in the kitchen," Bob said and I saw her pass before the window.

"She's a pretty girl," I said.

"You think so?" Bob asked, sounding surprised. "I never thought of her that way. She's always seemed like, oh, I don't know. Just Big Ed's wife, I guess."

We reached the house and Bob pulled open a groaning screen door. Ellen Nolan, standing at the sink, looked around.

"Hi, Ellen," Bob said and she smiled. "You haven't met Matt Harper, have you?"

"No, I haven't, Bob," Ellen said.

We smiled at each other.

"Ed tells me you're going to be our music director," she said.

"Yes." I nodded, thinking again how incredible it seemed that she was Ed Nolan's wife.

"That's wonderful," she said. Her brown eyes met mine as I heard Bob saying that we'd come down for a game of chess.

Ed Nolan was in the living room, talking sports with two of the athletic counselors.

"—play *hard* ball, *fast* ball." We got in on the tail end of his speech. "Teach 'em to *win*, not to lose. I don't go for this defeatist stuff, it makes a kid think in terms of winning or losing. If that's sportsmanship, you can have it." He glanced aside at us, then went on. "You teach a kid how to *win*; that's the American way. Play hard, play fast and *win*!"

He finished, his face reflecting satisfaction with his philosophy as he turned to us. He nodded curtly at Bob, extended his beefy hand to me.

"Haven't had a chance to talk to you man-to-man, Harper," he said. "Glad you dropped by, boy."

His bullish handshake sent needles of cutting fire into the raw flesh under my broken blisters and I couldn't keep the grimace from my face.

"What's wrong, boy?" he asked bluffly. "Too rough for ya?"

I told him it was blistered and he laughed. "Y'need a little toughenin' up," he said. "A summer's hard work'll do ya good. Sit down, boy, sit down."

"Could I get a drink of water first?" I asked, and he shrugged and pointed in the general direction of the kitchen. As I headed for it, I wondered why I'd said that. I wasn't thirsty at all. Maybe, I thought, I just wanted to get away from Nolan; or maybe I wanted to see Ellen Nolan again.

She was still at the sink, finishing up the dishes. She looked up with a friendly smile as I came in.

"May I get a drink?" I asked.

"Of course." She gestured toward a cupboard with her hand. "The glasses are up there."

As I stood close to her, running faucet water into the glass, I noticed, from the corners of my eyes, her looking at me. I turned to face her and she smiled quickly.

"Did your hands blister badly today?" she asked.

I nodded.

"Let me see," she said. She held my hand in her warm palm. "Oh, that looks terrible," she said concernedly. "You should have it treated."

"At the dispensary?" I asked.

"No, I have some ointment in the house," she said. "We can do it here."

"What's up, El?" Ed Nolan's voice inquired loudly as we came into the living room. When Ellen told him, he scoffed. "Aaah, that's nonsense. A few blisters never hurt anybody. Y'need toughening, boy."

"I know," I said politely, choosing concession as my guide to success with Big Ed Nolan. As I followed Ellen Nolan into the hallway, I heard Ed Nolan say to Bob, "You don't like sports, do you, Dalrymple?" and Bob's flustered, "Why...sure, sure I do, Ed. I'm not too good at them, of course, but—"

"Uh-huh," said Ed.

In the tiny bathroom, Ellen got boric acid ointment and a box of gauze.

"Go on in here," Ellen said, flicking on the bedroom light. "Sit down."

It gave me an odd sensation to sit on the bed beside Ellen Nolan. To hear her husband talking sports in the next room and see the picture of him, bulky in his football uniform, hanging over the bed with the pennant *Carlyle Teacher's College* tacked under it. To feel the careful touch of her fingers on my palm and watch her serious face as she put on ointment, then wrapped gauze around my hand and tied it.

"Like hers," I said without thinking.

She glanced up at me. "What?"

"Nothing," I said, "I was only...."

I didn't finish. I felt my heart thudding slowly, harshly. Her hands were like Julia's hands, warm and certain. I looked away from them.

"What sort of music will you teach the boys?" Ellen asked me.

"Oh, the usual run of camp songs," I said. "I've worked with kids before—at other camps—and they don't seem to like anything but the easiest songs."

She nodded. "I suppose so," she said. "It's a pity you can't give them a music appreciation course though. You know, play records and discuss them."

"Classical music?" I asked.

She nodded with a smile. "I think all people would like classical music if only they were exposed to it early enough," she said.

"You like it?" I asked.

"I love it," she said, "but my—" she hesitated for a revealing moment— "we don't have too many records," she finished.

"What do you have?" I asked.

"I'll show you when we're through," she said. "We have Tschaikowsky's—"

"What are ya doin', El?" Ed Nolan's voice came splashing over us like cold coffee and we both looked up to see him filling the doorway.

"I'm bandaging his hand, Ed," Ellen said as if she were apologizing.

"Well, come on out," he said irritably. "Our bedroom isn't a hospital, y'know."

Ellen Nolan's voice was barely audible as she said, "All right." I stood quickly, feeling restive under the flat gaze of Ed Nolan's eyes. For a moment, I hesitated between waiting to follow Ellen Nolan out and proceeding her. Then, as Ed stepped into the room and gestured once with his head, I moved abruptly for the doorway.

"We got a dispensary y'know," Ed said, attempting to sound amused but failing. "Our bedroom isn't no blister hospital."

I glanced over my shoulder and saw the tight look on Ellen Nolan's face, the rising color in her cheeks. Then I saw Ed Nolan pinch her as she moved past him. She gasped suddenly and lurched so bad she would have fallen if he hadn't caught her arm.

"Take it easy, El," said Big Ed, smirking. "You'll last longer."

He came out after her and saw me standing in the middle of the living-room floor. "Sit down, boy," he said.

"Mrs. Nolan said she was going to show me some records," I said.

"Never mind that," Ed said. "Sit down. I want to talk to you."

Without a word, I sat down beside Bob, as Ellen Nolan moved back toward the kitchen.

"What are your plans for singin' this summer?" Ed asked me. "I'll tell you right now I argued with the board against havin' a music director so I'm gonna expect mighty good work from ya before I'm convinced."

"Here's what I'm planning," I began.

As I spoke I could hear Ellen Nolan moving in the kitchen.

7.

"Tomorrow we're gonna work on the cabins," Ed Nolan told us at supper the next day, "and that's *all* we're gonna work on because I want those cabins in topnotch order by Wednesday morning when the camp-

25

ers arrive. Oh—" he conceded with a brusque gesture—"there may be a few odds and ends besides the cabins. A few of you cabin counselors may be assigned to other jobs but they'll only last an hour or so. Your main job'll be the cabins."

In the morning, Ed Nolan grabbed my arm as I was leaving the dining hall.

"Say, listen, boy, would you do me a favor?" he asked.

"Sure," I said. "What is it?"

"Well, we got all our work assigned for today but we're still a couple o' men short for helping clean up Paradise."

"Oh?" I said.

"I thought maybe you and Dalrymple might pitch in and help up there for a little while," said Big Ed.

"All right," I said. "I'll be glad to."

"I'll tell Doc Rainey then," he said. "Tell your friend Dalrymple."

"We'll still be able to work on our cabins today, won't we?" I asked as Bid Ed started away.

"Sure, sure," he tossed over his receding shoulder. "It'll just be for a little while."

When I told Bob about it, I saw the tightening of angry suspicion knit his features.

"That son-of-a-bitch is out to get us," he said. "He'll have us up there all day."

"If he does, he's cutting his own throat," I said. "He's the one who wants the cabins done by tomorrow morning."

"He'll expect them done by tomorrow morning too," Bob said.

For an hour we worked down the long, facing rows of toilets, Bob humming a minor transposition of "Stranger in Paradise," as he scrubbed and flushed and scrubbed again.

"There is beauty here," he announced once, straightening up, dripping brush in hand. "There is intangible loveliness, grace, symmetry — a formlessness of unspeakable glory."

"There is a strong odor," I conceded.

"Callow youth," he said sadly, "who do not see this moment in its true significance. *Hark.*" He flushed. "It is the rushing of a crystal stream, a torrent of summer madness. Ah, it is Niagara, Victoria!"

"It is a toilet flushing," I said, still cleaning.

"You miss the point, fellow," he said. "The moment escapes you." He belched echoingly.

"It is the horn of Rolande summoning Charlemagne," I said.

"You've got it," he said. "Sit on it." He sang, "*Once you have found it, never let it go. Once you have found it*—"

Morning passed. There was only one other person working with us —a limp-armed dishwasher from the kitchen who mopped at the floor as if he were playing shuffleboard. By dinnertime, Paradise was still not regained from a winter's neglect.

Ellen was in the dining hall when we got there.

All through the meal, she kept looking at the table, only twice looking up, seeing me, and quickly lowering her eyes. Near the end of the meal, while Ed was telling us how slowly he thought the cabins were getting done and how, by God, we had better get into high gear and clean them up if it took all night—I looked at Ellen again and this time she didn't lower her waiting eyes. Instead, there was a moment—it seemed long; it probably lasted three seconds—a moment in which her eyes almost spoke to me—asking me to understand.

"Let's tell Doc," Bob said when Ed's talk was done, chopping away my thoughts of her and bringing me back again to the little prison of present difficulties; namely, getting our cabins done.

We went over to Doc Rainey and told him.

"We'll never get our cabin ready if we don't start soon," Bob complained. "We haven't even touched them."

Doc Rainey nodded, his face understanding. "I'll talk to Ed," he said. "I'm sure we can get somebody up there so you can get your cabins ready."

We waited while he talked to Big Ed, watching Ed gesture with a stump of cigar, as he explained. Finally they came over to us.

"Look here, boys," Ed said, "I don't wanna get tough or anything but you got a job to do so let's stop belly-achin' and *do* it."

"What about our cabins, Mister Nolan?" I asked.

"Listen, Harper," he said, "you two should have finished up Paradise hours ago. You're just wastin' time. The sooner you get the job done, the sooner you'll get to your cabins."

Thus spurred on, we returned to Paradise. Jokes did not set in that afternoon. We worked as quickly and efficiently as possible, mopping the floors, cleaning the sinks, dusting the walls, putting in fresh bulbs, rolls of paper, bringing up supplies from the lodge—cleaner, disinfectant, paper, soap, etc.

By three-thirty I tossed my mop into the utility closet and said, "Come on, that's it. We'd better work on those damn cabins."

Sid came by as I finished prying the wooden planks from over the door and letting down the shutters.

"Jesus, you're just starting?" he asked, looking mildly pained.

I told him about Paradise.

"I know," he said. "I don't blame you but...oh, the hell." He pulled off his sweat shirt, got a pail of soapy water and a mop and started working on the cabin floor while I broomed cobwebs from the outside eaves, changed the bulb and got mattresses from the lodge.

At four-thirty, the swim period was honkingly announced. Sid looked at me questioningly.

"I'll keep working," I told him. "Might as well get the damn thing over with." He nodded and smiled briefly.

Nolan came by a few minutes later and stood on the porch steps, eating a candy bar and looking in.

"Got a long way to go," he said through a caramel and nut-filled mouth.

I managed not to say anything.

"Paradise in topnotch order?" asked Big Ed.

"Yes," I answered bluntly.

"I'll take a look later on." He chewed noisily on his candy bar. "Say, Goldberg, come down the office with me, will ya? I want to go over the list of your campers with ya and tell ya about them."

"Well...." Sid put down the mop. "Harper has a lot to do yet," he said.

"That's Harper's job, not yours," Big Ed said. "Come on."

Sid left the cabin, grabbing his sweat shirt from the big, gnarled stump in front of the cabin. I stood barefoot on the soap-swirled floor, mop handle in limp clutch, looking out of the cabin.

By supper I had the floors done, the bunks set up. That left only the painting of the shutters and the locating and lugging up from the lodge of the seven trunks that belonged to my cabin group.

Bob and I sat by Merv at supper, neither of us talking much.

"You both look shot," Merv said. "Like men back from the dead."

"We're not back yet," Bob said.

"Large Edward on your tail?" Merv asked me and I nodded. "This is a position you'll learn to assume automatically in time," he said amusedly. "After a while you won't even notice it."

"This I doubt," I said.

I looked for Ellen at supper but she was absent again. I decided to drop by the Nolan cabin later if I were finished working.

"Say, Harper," Big Ed said to me at the door, "I took a look at Paradise before." He shook his head. "It's kind o' sloppy, boy, not a topnotch job by a long shot."

"I'm sorry," I said, as evenly as possible.

Big Ed nodded patronizingly. "Well, we'll let it go this time, Harper. But you got to get in high gear. Counselin's no picnic, y'know."

"Yes," I said, "I know."

"Well, I won't keep ya from your work." He patted me on the shoulder. "Check ya later."

I spent the evening painting the shutters by flashlight. About eight-thirty, Big Ed lumbered by.

"*Now* it's getting done," he said. I grunted. "Don't forget the trunks," he said. "And, while you're at it you might as well go over the beams." He pointed up at the ceiling. "Looks like a lot o' dust up there."

"Yes," I said, "I will."

At ten I began lugging up the trunks. By ten-thirty I was done. I took a shower and got into my pajamas; turned out the light and crawled exhaustedly between the sheets.

I lay there in the darkness thinking about Julia. About our years together, our engagement, our wedding plans.

Her funeral.

I wondered when it was going to leave me — this cold, sickening despair. She was dead; buried. Face that, a friend had told me months before. Face it and you can live with it. Ignore it and it will kill you. It was killing me. Over a year had passed since the auto accident; and the gaping hole was still there in my life. Nothing seemed to mend it.

TWO

1.

The buses arrived a little after one that afternoon. Dinner had been served at eleven-thirty so we'd all be ready and tensed for the onslaught. From twelve-thirty on, we gathered in the open area in front of the dining hall, waiting.

About one o'clock, the first audible signs of the terrible approach reached our ears. Almost unnoticeably, the sound impinged, increasing in volume gradually like distant surf. The noise grew louder, louder and then, with a flash of yellow side and windows alive with arms and heads, the first thick-tired bus turned in off the road and a burst of cheering dinned in our ears.

Then the second bus turned in and the first one ground to a whining halt in from of the dining hall, ejecting a torrent of yelling boys carrying baseball hats, tennis rackets, bows and arrows, suitcases, inner tubes, footballs, dufflc bags, knapsacks and one book. The second bus drew up, braked and cascaded more little boys. Then the third bus, the fourth and, in a minute, the area was interwoven with the dashing and jumping of one hundred and twenty-six vari-sized campers. The air rang with their cheers, yells, hoots of recognition, and general noisemaking.

Which pandemonium faded only after Doc Rainey had whistle-blown his face to a mottled purple. Even then, movement did not cease but went on, a tireless series of wrigglings, hoppings, punchings of arms, ticklings, pokings and repressed gigglings.

"All right, now!" Doc Rainey's voice rose courageously above the squirming, bright-eyed throng. "Line up for cabin assignments!"

The initial attempt of the boys to carry out this instruction paralleled a meeting of two armies—the first composed of dogs, the second of cats. The feverish shrilling of Doc Rainey's whistle finally brought motionless silence to the red-faced, tangled gang.

"All right—*take it easy!*" Doc Rainey implored. "Slowly! Counselors, help! Line up everyone in two rows!"

After a sweat raising formation tactic, the boys finally stood in two wavering, occasionally cracking lines. Doc's whistle pierced the air again and the boys gulped down noise into themselves. Whereupon Doc called out each individual name and told them to go and stand with their counselor. Thus it was that in forty-five minutes, I had my seven boys standing around me—my Chester Wickerly, a pudgy, freckled-faced 6-B Cagliostro; my Moody brothers, Jim and Roger, both lean and wearing shorts, both chewing gum, both carrying identical tennis rackets; my Martin Gingold, short, fat, slickly black-haired and wearing a red sweat shirt bearing the awesome title—*172nd Street Eagles*; my David Lewis, a good-looking little boy with that scared and transparent expression of the boy who has never been away from Mama; Charles Barnett, a husky, self-assured towhead; and finally my Anthony Rocca, a skinny, pale-faced runt, staring big-eyed at everything going on, mouth slightly gaping, lugging over his shoulder a *Louisville Slugger* that would have given Babe Ruth trouble. My heavenly seven.

At Sid Goldberg's word, I led them to their summer home. In the cabin, they lunged for bunks and I had to separate the flailing Moody boys and make them flip a coin for upper berth. Jim won and a scowling Roger made up his lower bunk with angry, vengeful motions. I noticed how David Lewis watched, tremble-chinned, until the flurry over bunks had ceased and then, gingerly, took the remaining bunk. He put down his duffle bag and settled on the edge of the mattress looking around the cabin with an uncertain look on his face.

I sat on my bunk and watched them all while they made their beds, hung up hats, raincoats, Sunday pants, tennis rackets and fishing poles. I had to get up once to help David Lewis with his bunk. Finally, I sat down again and watched while they put on their bathing suits. David Lewis stayed on his bunk, looking around with timorous eyes while he changed, obviously embarrassed. The rest of them except for Tony Rocca stripped down with the casual aplomb of seasoned campers and had soon wriggled into their trunks. I noticed how skinny Tony Rocca was, getting the feeling that if he were put in front of a bright light, you could see through him.

Next came the physical. Barefoot and carrying towels, we all marched across the log bridge, past the dining hall and over to the line in front of the dispensary. An hour passed while the line edged toward the door and then we were inside, and Miss Leiber, gray-haired and curt, weighed, heighted, peered into ears, noses and throats, eye tested, took temperatures and generally examined. I noticed David Lewis shivering, on the verge of tears, and I put my hand on his shoulder. His cool skin twitched under my fingers and his eyes looked up fearfully at me.

"Nothing to be afraid of," I told him.

The rest of the cabin except for Tony Rocca took the examination in stride. Tony kept asking Miss Leiber, "What's that for, ma'am?" sort of distrustingly as each new part of his exam came up.

"To look at your ears with," Miss Leiber said.

"What's that for?"

"Your throat."

"What's that for?"

"Eyes."

Finally, she just grunted and performed the examination in wordless haste. After it was over, Tony Rocca walked beside me as we headed toward the lake for swimming tests.

"I wasn't scared when she stuck that stick in my mouth," he told me.

"No, of course not."

"Did you see that kid cryin'?"

"No."

"He was cryin' 'cause he was yella. I didn't cry."

"You're not yella."

"Damn right," he said.

The buoy-enclosed swimming area of the lake was white-spumed with splashing campers as we walked out onto the dock. The test for proof of swimming ability required a relatively serene trip out to the float and back again. Three rowboats sculled about en route, two counselors in each one, one rowing, the other with an oar, ready to haul in sputtering hopefuls who couldn't quite make it. Mack was one of them with an oar.

None of my first five boys had any trouble. They splashed out to the float and back with the assurance of Weismullers in the rough. Nor could it be said that David Lewis had any trouble. When his name was called he simply informed Jack Stauffer that he couldn't swim and was assigned to the Beginner's Group, which group practiced their paddling in the roped-off shallows.

All through the tests, Tony Rocca stood beside me shivering.

"I can swim," he kept assuring me, "I'm a good swimmer."

"Fine," I said.

"I ain't scared."

"Of course not," I agreed.

"I'm a good swimmer."

When his name was called, I saw the pupils of his eyes expand suddenly and, with a tightly twisted mouth, he lunged forward and flopped off the dock into the choppy water. He disappeared for a moment, then appeared on the surface, dark hair plastered over his forehead, arms and legs flailing as if he were fighting off a crocodile. Mack saw that it was obvious Tony couldn't swim and stuck the oar down for him.

Tony wouldn't take it. Gasping for air, swallowing mouthfuls of lake and gagging, he kept on, arms windmilling, legs kicking spastically at the water, then finally had to be dragged out.

"I can swim!" he yelled as they pulled him on the dock. "Leggo! I can swim, I can swim! God damn it, *leggo!*"

"Beginner," drawled Jack Stauffer, while Sid Goldberg lectured Tony on the subject of proper language.

When we left the dock, the other boys were laughing and Tony shivered and looked sick as he stumbled back up the hill to our cabin.

2.

On my way down to the Nolan cabin with Bob, Sid Goldberg stopped me for a moment. Bob went on while I sank down on the camp chair beside Sid. It was just getting dark.

"How's Tony Rocca getting along?" he asked me.

"Pretty good," I said. "He doesn't take care of his clothes, of course.

He eats like a starving longshoreman and he has rather an advanced vocabulary for one of his tender years. But, outside of that—"

Sid didn't smile back. He nodded his head slowly, looking out at the dark woods.

"I think you ought to know about Tony," he said. "Ed doesn't think I should tell you but—" he gestured vaguely with one hand—"well, this is strictly on the q.t."

"All right," I said, nodding once. "Anything you say."

"Tony's a charity case," Sid said. "The camp board is paying for his summer here."

"Oh?" I said, wondering if that was the dreadful secret.

Sid drew in a slow breath. "Tony spent last year in a mental institution," he said.

"No!"

He nodded sadly. "Tried to kill somebody."

"Who?" I asked.

"I don't know," he answered. "Ed didn't tell me. And I don't care. What counts is that we make the kid forget, see that he has a nice summer. I don't mean let him do anything he pleases; but—well, temper your discipline with a little extra understanding. In other words, handle him with kid gloves."

I sat there, wordlessly disturbed.

"That's about it," Sid said. "Don't worry about it. Just keep it in mind. It's something I think you should know."

"I think so too," I said. "Why in hell didn't Nolan *want* me to know."

"I don't know," Sid said. "He has his own ideas."

Not knowing just want Sid's relationship to Ed was, I let it go at that. I thanked him for telling me and then moved down the trail to Nolan's cabin.

I played chess with Bob. A few other counselors were sitting around the living room, reading, listening to jazz records and playing cards. Ellen didn't show herself once although I could hear her moving around behind the closed bedroom door.

Around ten-thirty there was a crashing of breaking glass from behind that door and we all started.

"What's that?" I heard myself ask.

"Guess she dropped a glass in the bathroom," Bob said. "Check."

I returned to the game, wondering why Ellen bothered me so. Was it because she was one among so many men? Miss Leiber was too old, Pat Stauffer too stuffy. Was it that look in her eyes? Or was it my mind, desperately seeking some way to forget Julia? I didn't know. I only know I couldn't concentrate on the game until I heard Ellen moving around in the bedroom again; heard the sound of her sitting down heavily on the bed.

"Checkmate," said Bob happily.

3.

God knows whatever happened to Tony's clothes. Sherlock Holmes could have gone stark, staring mad trying to keep track of them. After the first week I didn't even try. Once in a while, maybe, I'd find a tee-shirt lying in the woods or, rummaging through the lost-and-found pile in the back of the dining hall, come up with an armful of shorts, towels, washcloths, handkerchiefs, and socks. About the only things Tony kept track of were his bathing trunks and his baseball bat; the latter because it was his pride and joy, the former because he wore them almost twenty-four hours a day and couldn't very well lose them short of walking around naked.

To make it worse, those clothes that managed, somehow, to stay

within the vicinity of the cabin were all monstrously dirty. I'd keep telling him to wash them.

"Just a little bit every day, Tony," I'd say. "That way there's no trouble
at all." Big eyes staring blankly. "But the way you let it all pile up—"
Grave shake of Counselor Harper's graying head, attempt by Counselor
Harper to look effectively grim. All useless. Tony went to the ball field.
Tony went to the lake. Tony read comic books and made a bead ring at
the craft shop but Tony never washed clothes.

The other kids in the cabin went more or less regularly up to Paradise with armfuls of grimy wardrobe, washed them in a sink with soap
chips provided by the camp, hung them in the sunshine, then put them
away in their trunks, if not clean at least sweeter smelling. Tony paid no
attention. It got to the dismal point where his only apparel, outside of
the bathing trunks, was a pair of dirty white ducks and a dirtier red
sweater. After the second Sunday service he wore this outfit, Ed Nolan
cornered me with the decree to "get him on the ball," "get him in high
gear" and thus and so.

So, the next day—Monday of the third week, I wouldn't let Tony
out of the cabin. Almost forcibly, I removed the enormous bat from his
shoulder, peeled off his cap and sat him down solidly on his bunk.

"Today we wash, Tony," I said, adding quickly as he stared to argue,
"But me no buts, Anthony. We *wash*."

"But I got a *series* game, Matt!"

I knew that Tony was, to put it mildly, imagining things. Usually he
went to the ball diamond, shillelagh bobbing over gaunt shoulder, then
sat there on the bench and watched, the bat end resting on the ground
between his feet, held like an old man's cane. Once in a while, maybe,
some desperate boy would ask Tony to have a catch with him. Even less
frequently, some team would be so far behind in runs that they'd let him

play outfield where he'd have one hell of a time dropping every flyball that came to him, grinning widely at the groans of his teammates and firing the ball back with a vigorous dispatch—usually over third base onto the road.

I stood unmoved and adamant. He struggled at first with many a "But *Matt*" and a "I *gotta!*" thrown in to bolster his struggle to quit the cabin. I persevered, however, and, finally, failing with the overt method, Tony slumped on his side on the bunk and stared at the wall, occasionally dropping a phrase which, although muttered under breath, still managed to reach me.

"All right, never mind the cussing," I said. "Your clothes are filthy. You are a disgrace to the good name of Cabin Thirteen. You will *wash*."

And, with that, I laid the behemoth bulk of his laundry bag by his side.

"Come on now," I said, "either you wash or I go get Sid."

Tears in his great, confused eyes; a curl to his lips.

"I know," I said, "you're in beautiful agony. Now are you going to wash your clothes?"

"I got a *series!*" Vehemently; voice of the betrayed.

I left to get Sid. When we returned to the cabin, it was empty. The laundry bag was gone too.

"Well, either he dumped it in the lake or he's washing," I judged.

We found him in Paradise, surrounding by mountains of dirty clothes, cursing heartily while he scrubbed at the sink. As Sid and I entered, the cursing stopped and the scrubbing increased a little. When we reached the sink Tony looked up at Sid with sorrowful pleading in this eyes.

"Gee, Sid, I got a *series* game."

"Tony, until you learn to take care of your clothes, you can't expect to play ball."

Silence, then scrubbing and a muffled, "Don't know why I came to this lousy goddam camp anyway."

I left, hearing, as the screen door closed behind me, those familiar lines from Sid, "Now, look, Tony. Matt is only doing this for your own good." And the sullen reply, "I know."

Later, I returned and found miles of clothes hanging on the lines beside Paradise. None of them were clean, of course, but they were all wet anyway. I felt that was the most I could ask on such short notice.

When I reached the cabin, Tony was just coming out with his bat.

"I'm sorry, Matt," he said. "I'll try better. I'm gonna wash a little clothes every day and then it won't pile up."

"That's fine," I managed. "That's the stuff, Tony."

"Ain't that the best, Matt? A little clothes every day?"

"Sure. That's the best, Tony."

He left for his imaginary series game, leaving me in pleasant shock. After less than two weeks, a slight change for the better. He was sorry. He was going to "try better." It made me feel very good.

After dinner, came the balancing act.

Toward the end of the rest period, Mulhausen of Cabin 14 pushed the old wheelbarrow up the hill from the lodge, stopped in front of each cabin and tossed a stack of letters on the face of the poor counselor who was trying to catch a little sleep after knocking himself out for fifty minutes trying to keep the kids quiet.

I handed out the letters that particular day, noticing that there was one from Tony's mother. It was the first letter he'd received since camp started and it pleased me to watch him settle down on his bunk and, excitedly, tear open the envelope.

The cabin was quiet for a few moments as it could only be when the boys were absorbed either in mail or comic books. Then began the inevitable comments.

"Oh boy!" (From Charlie Barnett) "My mom is sending me two suits. I'm gonna go to the dance next week."

"I'm gettin' my new shirts and my brown sport coat!" (From Marty Gingold)

"My dad is sending me five bucks!" (Chester Wickerly)

Tony very quiet, reading, then looking up excitedly.

"Oh boy! My mom is sending me my blue suit and some shirts and some pants and everything!"

His remark went unnoticed as did all the rest. The boys didn't really expect any reception from their little personal remarks. They just wanted to let these things be known.

Shortly after, the dock horn squalled and afternoon activity officially began. Bathing suits replaced shorts, tennis rackets and ball bats ousted comic books, forced repose succumbed to violent movement. In a minute, the last of the boys had dashed out of the cabin with Tony, as usual, trudging off to the diamond, weighed down by the *Louisville Slugger* that was almost as long as he was.

I finished my mail—a letter from my mother and one from a friend—and went to the door, stretching. Maybe an ice cream now.

Then an urge; unkind, if you will. I suddenly wanted to read Tony's letter. I wanted to see what his mother was like, I wanted to see if there was any hint in her words of the warped debilities she had transferred to her son. Was she young, wild, irresponsible? Or old, stolid, ignorant? I knew that Tony's father had divorced her; Sid had told me that. But that was all I knew.

I sat down on Tony's bunk and picked up the letter.

I hope you're enjoing yourself. I hope you'll be good. I hope I can come and see you. I hope you lisen to your counsiler. (A smile from me.)

I sat there. I read that letter again, not understanding. Where was "the blue suit and some shirts and some pants and everything?" I kept rereading the letter, not quite able to believe it, undergoing a strange, unrealistic feeling; one I had trouble adjusting to.

There it was though. A ten-year-old boy who had to lie because there was nothing else to balance himself with. A little boy who could find equality only in imagining.

I didn't know what to do or think. I couldn't tell Tony; I wouldn't want him to know I'd read his letter. There was nothing to do, nothing to say. Just keep quiet, be a little ashamed for knowing and three cheers for people who breed children only to ruin them.

4.

It was dark in the cabin; early morning. Everyone should have been asleep but I heard a moaning. I sat up with a rustling of bedclothes and listened hard.

Tony.

Realizing that, I suspected for a moment that it was a trick since he was excessively prone to them at all hours. I sat there listening a moment to see if he'd cease crying midnight wolf.

He didn't. The moaning went on and I got up and went over to his bed with my flashlight. I shone it down a little to the side of his face and saw his eyes, wide and stricken.

"What's the matter, Tony?" I asked quietly.

"My foot hurts."

I pulled aside the army blanket and shone my flashlight there. It was no wonder his foot hurt. It was swollen and inflamed, along the bottom of it a ragged gash, purple-edged with infection.

"Good God, when did *this* happen?"

"Couple days ago."

"*How?*"

"I...j-jumped offa the dock and landed on a rock."

"Well, why didn't you tell somebody?"

"I was scared."

No answer to that; it was beyond argument. I could only care for him. As gently as I could, wincing along with him, I wrapped some gauze from my first-aid kit around the foot and told him we'd go to the dispensary in the morning.

"You've got to *tell* people when you get hurt, Tony," I said. "Don't keep it a secret."

Only a sniffling and a tear from Tony Rocca. I felt a sudden rush of pity for the kid. My smile was as tender as a smile in the sleep-logy middle of the night can be.

"It's all right, Tony," I said. "All right. Go to sleep now."

"Thanks, Matt." Quietly and gratefully.

I went back to my bed and lay awake awhile to see if he was going to be all right. He made no further sounds of pain and, after about fifteen minutes, I heard the delicate babbling of his snores. I turned on my side, amused at the parental feeling I had.

The next morning I took Tony to the dispensary where I spent an hour or so with him, lending moral support while a scolding Miss Leiber lanced, drained, sulfa-powdered and bandaged. When we finally returned to the cabin, Tony had a slipper on his bad boot and he made a pathetic picture limping back to the cabin with his *Louisville Slugger* for a cane.

A few nights later, I woke up and heard him sobbing. With a head-shaking sigh, I slipped out of bed and went over to him.

"What now, little man?" I said. No answer. I pulled up his blanket again and pointed the flashlight beam at the foot. Which lay, unbandaged and dirty on the course blanket.

"What did you do with your bandages?" I asked in an angry mutter.

More silence. I shined the flashlight into his big, helpless eyes.

"Well? What did you take them off for? Good God, haven't you got any more sense than that?"

"I wanted to look at it."

"Ohhhh...*Gawd*!"

I found the bandage coiled on the floor like a gauzy serpent and, tearing off the part that had gotten dirty, I re-bandaged the foot. It was inflamed again and Tony had to grit his teeth as I bandaged.

"For God's sake, cry if you want to," I muttered grumpily.

"Don't want to." His voice was thin and shaky but resolute.

When I'd finished, I shined the light to the side of his face.

"Now *look*," I snapped. "Leave it alone! How do you expect it to get better if you play with it?"

"Whassat? Whassat?" came a befuddled query from the semiconscious Chester Wickerly, wild man and wind breaker of Cabin 13.

"Go to sleep," I ordered, returning to my bed, tripping over Chester's sneaker in so doing. I cursed and kicked the sneaker across the floor, seriously questioning my sanity in taking a counselor's job for the summer.

For the next few days, Tony was pretty well behaved. I don't count him limping down to the lake to fish and falling in. That was in a day's expectation. What I mean is—he left the new bandage intact and didn't try to play baseball.

Though, as a matter of fact, it was all I could do to keep him from running off on Cabin 13's first hike day (each cabin had four during the two-month season). It was painfully obvious that Tony was in no condition for hiking but that didn't seem to worry him. His obliviousness to the demands of the flesh bordered on lunacy.

"Look," I said, practically sitting on his chest, "your foot is bandaged. It's infected. The way you've been treating it, you're lucky you can get around at *all*. But you cannot walk for miles on it under a hot sun!"

"Aw, gee, Matt, I could hop on my good foot, couldn't I?"

"*No!*"

His face curled up, blossom-like, and I had to resort to quiet, well-modulated reason. Arm around his match-stick shoulders, voice a soothing monotone, I said, "Stay in camp, Tony. You've got lizards and frogs to chase, ball games to watch, comic books to read, crafts to work on and a great big lake to fall in."

"Oh...sh—"

"Aah-aah."

"*Shoot.*"

I grinned at him. After a moment, he grinned back. "Diablo," I said.

"So's your old man," he countered.

He lay on his bunk that afternoon, I remember, game foot propped up on the window sill, fingers picking out mattress stuffing from the bunk above. I was working out a musical program for the first campfire songfest and pow-wow which was coming up in a few days. My music directing, as yet, hadn't really been put to the test except for some songs during movie-reel changing on Wednesday nights and for hymns on Sunday.

While I worked, Tony sang his favorite song. He sang it often in his frail voice and, sometimes, I thought there was a kind of simile between the song and his life.

"There was a little mouse lived on a hill
      —mmm-*mmm*, mmm-*mmm*
There was a little mouse lived on a hill
      —mmm-*mmm*, mmm-*mmm*
There was a little mouse lived on a hill
As rough and tough as Buffalo Bill
      —mmm-*mmm*, mmm-*mmm*."

That was the opening verse which broke the ground for endless more in which this versatile rodent disported himself through varied, fantastic adventures, touching foot upon strange shores, accosting, in his mousy arrogance, a veritable galaxy of weird and fascinating characters ranging from Miss Mousy (who, it is noted, spurned his marital advances) and so on up all the way to The Rat That Sat on a Big Black Rock.

There was another song too but I didn't like that one. It started:

One night I heard an awful noise
I looked up on the wall
The bedbugs and the cockroaches
Was havin' a game o' ball.

It was a song Tony had picked up at the mental institution; a song that was based upon actuality. That song gave me a hideous feeling. For there is something infinitely more terrible about a child being lost than an adult; and that song kept reminding me that, unless someone intervened, Tony might well be lost.

I was only going to be with him for two months and what were two months in a lifetime? All the harm that had been done before he came to Camp Pleasant I couldn't hope to undo in such a short time. All the things that had scarred and stained his mind could only be cleared away by a long-range miracle. Sometimes I visualized his probable future and it didn't make me smile or want to smile.

Little Tony. Needing someone so desperately, yet never finding that someone. Always with that unconscious look of hungry yearning on his face—yearning for a hope that kept moving ahead of him, flitting like a cruel shadow, always mocking, always unattainable.

5.

We sat in a small clearing in the woods, a thin wisp of fire smoke climbing toward the sky like a gray snake elevating to a fakir's fluting. Merv, the boys and I sat absorbed in beans and frankfurters which had been burned to a turn by Chef Wickerly.

"On the surface I agree with you," Merv was telling me. "To come back here and be exposed year after year to Ed Nolan *is* idiocy. However, as I told you, I do like the camp, always have. I like my position in it. I'm not responsible for anything but hikes and I like hiking.

"Of course," he admitted, "if it gets much worse, even *I* won't be able to stand it any more. It's a pity, really. Pleasant is a fine camp; its personnel isn't so bad; but that gluttonous fascist louses up the whole deal."

"What do you know about Nolan's wife?" I asked, hoping I wasn't making a mistake.

"A very strange young woman," he said, chewing reflectively. "I've been here five years and I still don't know her. Not that I've had much contact with her of course. The first year or so I spoke to her. We talked about music, books, plays, all sorts of things. Things which she's starved for as the wife of we know who."

I nodded.

"Naturally, as soon as said Ed grew aware of the talks, he squelched them." Merv tossed the paper plate of beans onto the fire. "She was quite pleasant too," he said.

"I know."

We were silent a moment, then I asked him if he knew how old she was.

"Let's see, I think she told me. Oh...." He tapped his teeth with one long nail. "I think she's about twenty-six."

"She doesn't look it."

"Hadn't noticed," said Merv.

"Is there anything wrong with her?"

"Just a massive neurotic depression bordering on psychosis," Merv said, casually. "Who can blame her, married to that pig?"

"Why in hell did she marry him then?" I heard myself asking in more than normal irritation.

"The details aren't important," Merv said. "The basic reason seems obvious enough, however. She couldn't do any better."

"That's ridiculous," I said. "She's a lovely girl."

Merv looked at me with quick curiosity which was, just as quickly, repressed.

"Well," was all he said, "she's still married to him."

"Yes, she is," I said.

"What about you?" Merv changed the subject. "What brings you here?"

"I don't know," I admitted. "I suppose I came for lack of anything better to do. Bob's been after me for years to try it."

"You knew him in college, didn't you?" Merv asked.

"That's right," I said. "We've seen each other off and on since we graduated."

"What do you do the rest of the year?" Merv asked.

"Work in a music store," I said.

"Uh-huh." Merv nodded. "You have a girl?"

I tossed my plate on the fire. "She's dead," I told him.

"What happened?" he asked.

"Auto accident," I said. "Collision. She died the next morning."

"Oh, I'm sorry, Matt."

I grunted. "We were going to be married in a week when it happened," I said.

"Oh, no." Merv looked pained.

"Yep." I nodded. "I was going to work in her father's plant. Big executive type. We had all our furniture, a house picked out, a car—" I stopped and exhaled heavily. "That was the car she was killed in," I said.

We sat quietly, looking into the fire.

"I'm sorry I made you talk about it, Matt," he said then.

"I guess I should talk about it more," I answered. "That's what they keep telling me."

6.

Sid met me in front of the dining hall when we got back from the hike. "Tony," was all he said.

"*No*," I said, fearing the worst. "What happened?"

"He fell on top of a bottle and it broke. Cut his hand and wrist all to hell."

"Badly?"

"He had to have six stitches."

"Oh...dear God! Where is he?"

"The dispensary."

Tony was lying on a cot when I got there, turning comic book pages with his good hand. He didn't see me at first and I stood looking at the bulky taped-down windings around his hand and wrist and the ones around his foot. I looked at the intent expression on his thin face as he followed The Batman through various exigencies of plot.

"Hello, sad sack," I finally said.

He looked up quickly, smiled. "*Hi*, Matt. I cut myself."

"So I've been told," I said. "Couldn't leave you alone one day, could I?"

"Aw, gee, Matt," he said earnestly, "it wasn't *my* fault. Some guy shoved me."

"Who?"

"I dunno. Down at the store."

"Tony, Tony," I said, "what are we going to do with you?"

"Hey, Matt, will you tell the old lady nurse I can go swimmin' this afternoon?"

"No, Tony," I shook my head wearily. "You cannot go swimmin' this afternoon."

"Aw, *gee*, Matt!"

As I stepped out of the dispensary cottage, I almost bumped into Ellen.

"Hello," I said.

She smiled. "Hello, Matt."

"It's been a long time since I've seen you."

"Yes," she answered, her smile a little less convincing now, "it has."

"How have you been?"

"Oh...fine. How have *you* been?"

"Swell." I nodded, smiling, and we stood in awkward silence a moment.

"Well...." she started, as if preparing to leave.

"I was just in to see Tony Rocca," I said hastily, not wanting her to go.

"The little boy who cut himself?"

I nodded. "He wants to go swimming," I told her.

She smiled, "They never have any sense at that age, do they?"

"Never," I said, smiling back.

Another silence.

"Well, I guess I'd better be getting along," she said.

I didn't want her to go but all I could do was smile, say, "All right," and step aside. I watched her walk away.

Later I had a swim with Bob, during which we discussed Merv. "If you ever get a chance, ask him to come to your cabin some night and tell the kids horror stories," Bob told me.

"Maybe I will," I said. "I'm running out of stories."

"Oh, Christ, Merv isn't," Bob said. "He makes them all up." He chuckled to himself.

"Maybe I'll ask him tonight," I said. "There's a free bunk in the cabin by dint of T. Rocca's indisposition."

"I heard about that," Bob said. "He's a little bastard, isn't he?"

"No," I said, "just a lost soul."

We were silent then and, as Bob dived into the water to sidestroke around, I lay back in the lowering sunlight and stared up at the still blue of the sky, watching the cottony clouds move across my line of vision, feeling the cool water lap gently at my ankles, thinking of a beautiful girl I was going to marry before an automobile collision tore the life from her.

Supper time. The usual gabbles and giggles and little boys stuffing stomach cavities. And, in the middle of the main course, Big Ed rising, belching, waiting, speaking.

"You all know what happened this afternoon," he said. "And you all know *why. Rough*housin', that's why." He looked around the dining hall. "Anybody wants to roughhouse, send him to me. I'll give him a little roughhouse where it counts—on the *butt* with a canoe paddle! I don't want no shovin' or roughhousin' in my camp, ya understand? If it happens again, there's not gonna *be* any store open after rest period."

Again his eyes moved over us all, his cheeks puffing out gassily. "That's all," he said, surprising us with his untypical brevity. My meat loaf was still warm on my plate. And still warm in my stomach when Big Ed met me at the door and suggested I join him in the office.

"I guess you know what happened to Rocca this afternoon," he said.

I looked at him curiously, "Yes," I said, "I—"

I stopped talking as Ed Nolan jabbed a thick forefinger at me. "Harper, you're gonna have to get on the ball," he said. "That's the second time he's been to the dispensary this week."

"I know, but—"

"If you can't take care of your boys, Harper, I'll have to find someone who *can*."

I gaped. "You mean you're holding me responsible for what happened this afternoon?"

A slight, glowing flush moved up Big Ed's portly cheeks. "That's right," he said.

"But I wasn't even in *camp* this afternoon!"

"What in hell's *that* got to do with it?" Big Ed snapped. "Ya think you're not responsible for your kids soon as ya can't *see* them?"

"I don't understand, Mister Nolan," I said. "I took six of my boys on a hike this afternoon. I *had* to leave Tony Rocca behind because of his foot. How could I have anything to do with—"

"I don't like your attitude, Harper," he said. "You're not gonna last long here with an attitude like that."

Repressing anger sent a shudder down my back.

"I'm sorry," I said. "I'm not trying to argue with you, Mister Nolan. I just can't understand how I can be held responsible for every move my—"

"Well, ya *better* understand it!"

Another shudder. "All right," I said.

"That's all Harper," Big Ed cut the interview short. "Just remember I got my eye on ya, boy. Either you get in high gear or you're gonna find yourself out on your ass. Now, beat it, I'm busy."

Holding back words which would have ended my Camp Pleasant career posthaste, I left the office and went out of the dining hall.

7.

Reaching *The Crossroads Tavern* involved a four-mile walk south down the road from camp. It was one of three buildings, the other two being the *Shady Haven Motel—10 Cabins—TV in Every Room—Light Housekeeping* and *The Bramblebush Restaurant*, vintage 1920, an old converted home with heavy beamed ceilings, paneled walls and a stone fireplace. From the upper dining deck of the restaurant, you could see glinting flashes of the lake along whose south shore that road was constructed.

Bob and I were sitting in one of the tavern booths that night, drinking bottled beer and discussing, among other things, the annual Counselor Takeoffs in which everyone and everything fell before the truncheoning of lampoon, especially the upper echelon boys.

"This we must take loving care with," I said. "I must confess I would like to see Big Ed skinned alive."

Bob blew out more smoke. "I see you're finally coming around to our way of thinking," he said.

"Well, let's get back to the show," I said.

"Right," he agreed. "I think I've just about talked Sammy Wrazalowsky into playing Big Ed."

A heartfelt chuckle rumbled in my chest. Sammy Wrazalowsky was a gigantic butterball who taught ring-making in the craftshop.

"He may chicken out," Bob said. "But I think he'll do it."

"It is a role he was born to," I said.

"Gawd, can't you just see him in a tee-shirt full of holes?" Bob word-pictured. "His belly overlapping the belt of his low-slung trousers, a soda bottle in one hand, a sandwich in the other, ranting—'Get in high gear, get in high gear!'?"

"Can see," I admitted and a laugh most uncharitable ballooned above our booth.

We were discussing the possibility of setting up a stage by pushing together the square dining-hall tables when a young man leaned over our table.

"Pardon me, fellows," he said, "but are you from the boys' camp?"

We looked up. He had brown hair slicked down carefully, a red silk sport shirt, camel's-hair jacket over it, a cigarette inserted in a dark holder completing the picture.

We told him we were from the boys' camp.

"Do either of you know Merv Loomis?" he asked then.

"Yes, we know him," I said.

"Do you know where he is tonight?"

"In camp, I imagine," Bob said.

"Oh." The young man straightened up, visibly crestfallen. "Well," he said, "I thank you, gentlemen. If you see Merv, would you—oh, well, never mind."

"We see him every day," Bob said. "If you want us to give him a message.... "

Eyebrows raised, drooped. "Well," he pondered gingerly a moment, "just tell him that Jackie was asking for him, will you?"

The young man smiled pleasantly, turned away and walked down the row of booths.

"Sure thing, Jackie," I said to the air. "We'll tell him."

Bob and I exchanged a look. "Ooh, mama," he said.

I blew out breath slowly. "Let's not think about it," I said. "We've already decided we don't care about Merv's personal life. As far as I'm concerned, that still goes."

"I know." Bob pressed out his cigarette, a worried look on his face. "It's disturbing, though I guess I never really thought about Merv that way. I guess I was always so much on the defensive against the attitudes of guys like Mack and Ed that...well, that I never stopped to think they might be right."

"No." I shook my head. "Even if Merv is a homosexual, Mack and Ed are not right."

Bob nodded concedingly and we skipped the subject, returning to the discussion of the Counselor Takeoffs.

Two hours later, when we reached the camp, even the occasional appearance of the moon between cloud rifts had stopped.

"You going to bed?" Bob asked me, as we entered the camp grounds.

"I guess so," I said. "Why?"

"No reason. I...thought we might have a game of chess before bed."

I shook my head. "Not tonight, Bob," I said. "I don't want to take the chance of seeing Fat Eddie's porcine face any more today."

"Okay," Bob said.

It was he who saw the flashlight down on the dock as we started over the log bridge. He called my attention to it and we both stopped to look.

"I wonder what's going on down there?" he said. In the night air we could hear a faint sound of voices. They sounded angry.

"Let's go see," I said and, without another word, we recrossed the bridge and moved slowly down the hill. We could see the flashlight beam wavering back and forth down there and, as we drew closer, we saw who was standing in the light of it.

"It's Merv," Bob said quickly. "Oh, my God, he's—"

Naked. He was standing on the dock boards looking as outragedly dignified as he could wearing only lake water on his body. Bob and I stopped.

"—expect me to believe *that*?" we heard the voice of the man holding the flashlight.

Ed.

Bob and I moved out of the open and into a dark clump of trees near the lake edge.

"Why *shouldn't* I go swimming when I choose?" Merv was asking in a failing belligerence.

"Nobody goes swimmin' without nothin' on in *my* camp," Ed answered roughly, obvious satisfaction in his voice. "No use arguin' with me, Loomis. You're through."

A blank look of shock crossed Merv's spotlighted face. His voice became almost inaudible.

"*Through?*"

"You heard me," Ed said.

Then I noticed another shadow which, up till then, had been hidden behind the bulk of Ed Nolan. I couldn't make out who it was though.

"Now, one *moment*," Merv said, his voice rising nervously, "I told you I left my bathrobe here on the dock. I did *not* come walking down here like this."

"Where is it then?" asked Ed Nolan. "Did it fly away?"

"Maybe it was *taken* away," Merv said tensely.

"Oh, don't give me that," said Ed.

"Listen, I'm telling you that—"

"I'm not interested in what you got to tell me, Loomis," Ed interrupted. He pointed the flash beam toward shore, then back. "Come on. Get off this dock. You got fifteen minutes to clear outta my camp."

"Fifteen—!"

"You heard me!"

"Now, wait a *moment*," Merv insisted. "You can't—"

Ed grabbed Merv's arm and shoved him toward shore. "Get *movin'*, boy," he said, his voice thick with menace. "You haven't a leg t'stand on. Goldberg and I both saw you."

I heard Sid say, "But, Ed, I—"

"No buts about it," Ed cut in. "I'm not havin' no pervert in *my* camp."

"Listen, I don't have to take this—" Merv started.

"I said fifteen minutes!" Ed snapped. "If you're not out by then, I'll *throw* you out!"

"Are you actually—"

"*Get!*" Ed shoved at Merv's back and Merv went stumbling forward, slipping to one knee on the wet boards. "*Get up!*" Ed roared.

"Take it easy, Ed," Sid tried to calm him.

I felt my stomach muscles tightening as they started off the dock. I saw Ed flash the light beam at Merv's buttocks.

"Now ain't he *cute*," he said, his voice low and vicious.

Merv's head snapped around suddenly as he glared at Ed, the bright light splashing up his rigid features.

"That's enough of that," he said in a voice that trembled with anger.

"Oh, that's enough, is it?" Ed started forward until Sid grabbed his arm.

"Take it *easy*, Ed," he cautioned.

"No damn pervert's gonna talk to *me* like that," Ed answered.

Now the tall gauntness of Merv Loomis came walking past a few yards away from us and Bob and I held our breath, standing very still. I was thinking about the disappearance of Merv's bathrobe. It bothered me; almost as much as it bothered me that Ed should just happen to be on the dock with a flashlight as the bathrobe disappeared. Ed and Sid walked by next and we heard Sid trying to talk Ed out of throwing Merv out of camp and Ed's stubbornly angry reply—more than loud enough for Merv to hear—

"Naw. Naw. I'm not havin' any damn pervert in *my* camp. Use your brains, Goldberg. With all these kids, I'm s'posed to let someone like *him* loose? Takin' 'em on hikes? Bein' alone in the *woods* with 'em? What kind o' thinkin' is *that*, Goldberg?" The light flashed up. "Keep movin', Loomis!"

"Ed, he's been here for five years," Sid argued. "If anything was going to happen, don't you think it would have—"

"There's always a first time," said Ed Nolan sternly. "Always a first time. No, I'm sorry, I'm sorry. I don't like to fire nobody any more than you would. But my job is takin' care of these kids and if I let this jaybird stay, I wouldn't be doin' my job. You saw it, Goldberg, you saw him swimmin' naked and no clothes around at all."

The three of them moved into the night.

"Jesus Christ," I heard Bob mutter slowly.

"Well..." I swallowed. "He's got him. Right where he wants him."

We stood in silence a moment.

"What'll we do?" Bob asked then. "Go back to our—"

"No," I broke in. "I want to see it. I want to remember."

Without a word, Bob followed me along the shore and up toward the edge of the clearing where the cabin was that slept the craft shop counselors, the kitchen help and Merv.

As we approached the clearing edge, we saw the cabin light flare on and the loud complaints of the sleepy counselors. Complaints which were cut off instantly when they saw a lake-dripping Merv Loomis grabbing a towel from a coat hanger and Ed Nolan framed in the doorway.

"What's up?" I heard Mick Curlerman ask in a thin voice.

Ed paid no attention. "Come on, get your clothes on, boy," he ordered as Merv hastily dried himself.

"I have to—"

"Boy, you heard me," Ed told him. "You better be out o' here in time."

Merv's face was terrible in the bald cabin light. I'd never seen him without his glasses before; his eyes had that strange cast badly myopic eyes have in the absence of glasses. There was no color in his face except for purplish-looking lips. I thought he was sick for a moment until I realized that he'd been forced to walk naked and wet in the cold night air. I noticed for the first time how badly he shivered.

"Snap it up," Ed ordered. Merv dressed quickly, his lips pressed together, his eyes looking fixedly at the floor.

"And what's *that*, Loomis?" Ed Nolan demanded, pointing his flashlight toward Merv's bunk.

Merv's terrycloth bathrobe and Merv's towel.

"You wore it down to the lake, hanh?" Ed sneered. "I always knew you were a damn *liar*."

Merv stared blankly at the bathrobe. "But—" His cheek twitched. "I swear to God I—"

"Never mind," Ed snapped, "I'm not interested. Come on, come on, get dressed!"

"I tell you I wore that bathrobe down to the lake!"

"And I said get dressed!"

Merv shook badly as he finished putting on his clothes but no more than I did. It made my stomach turn to stand there looking at his confused expression as he dressed in jerky, erratic motions.

"Son-of-a-bitch" I heard Bob whisper, almost in a gasp.

Merv finished putting on a sweater and looked up dazedly at Ed.

"Awright, get your stuff together," Ed told him.

"But how—"

"Loomis, I'm not here t'argue with ya. Either you get your stuff out o' here or *I* will."

The scene went on, endless in its horror, silent except for the creak of the floor boards as Merv moved around nervously, pulling clothes off hangers, folding them hastily, putting them into his trunk.

"Come on, come on," Ed said impatiently, "I ain't got all night."

"I'm trying as—"

"Never mind the lip. Just *pack*."

Merv finished packing.

"Awright," Ed said. "Pick it up and let's go."

Merv stared at him blankly. "But I can't," he said. "It's too—"

"Ya want it tossed in the lake!" Ed snapped.

Merv bent over the trunk, his lips pressed together tightly. He tried to lift the big trunk but he couldn't. He managed to get one corner up but even that slipped. He looked up in fright as Ed Nolan cursed loudly and lunged into the cabin. Then he backed off as Ed grabbed up the trunk as if it were a small, empty suitcase. Ed spun on sneakered soles and banged through the doorway, ordering over his shoulder, "Grab the rest of your things and come on!"

"What are you going to do with my trunk?" Merv asked in a panicky voice but Ed didn't answer.

Sid went up the steps and into the cabin. "He's just taking it up to the road, Loomis," he said.

"But he said—"

"I know, I know," Sid said quickly. "He won't though. Come on, let's go."

I stood there numbly watching Sid help Merv gather up the rest of his things—a duffle bag of clothes, a small suitcase, a portable typewriter and some books. I saw how he avoided Merv's eyes, I saw how his mouth was as tight and thin as Merv's. Then they were out of the cabin and, as Merv started up the path, Sid turned in the doorway.

"Listen," he told them in a quick, clipped voice, "I don't want a word of this to get out, do you understand? Anyone who talks out of turn will have me on his tail the rest of the season. I'm not kidding."

He snapped off the lights and went down the steps quickly, then around the cabin and up the path toward the road.

We didn't say anything or plan anything but, as if it were prearranged, Bob and I moved off and started along the patch of woods that sides the path. Before we reached the road, I heard a loud, crunching sound and knew that it was Ed tossing down the trunk on the pavement.

"Awright," we heard him say, "now get outta my camp and *stay* out."

"What about my s-salary?" Merv asked.

"You'll get your check when the time comes," Ed said disgustedly. "Now clear out." His voice became sickeningly cute. "Or maybe you want t'kiss your *boy* friends good-bye first."

Merv's long face turned to stone.

"You *muck-minded swine*," he said slowly and clearly, the words dripping like acid. "Is there anything but utter filth in that mind of—"

He broke off nervously and backed away as Ed started forward.

"I'd take that back," he said, "*queer.*"

"Why *should* I?" Merv asked, his scorn weakened. "I don't work for you any more, remember?"

"Ya gonna apologize?" The sound in Ed Nolan's voice was terrifying.

"No, I'm not!" Merv backed off more.

It happened too quickly for Sid to prevent it. One second Merv was edging away from Ed, the next second Ed had him by the right arm and was driving a bunched fist into his face. A stunned gasp of pain burst from Merv as he went flailing back, fell over his trunk and landed on the pavement heavily. Ed moved at him again but Sid caught his arm.

"Ed, for God's sake!"

"Let go my arm!" Ed cried in a mindless, croaking voice. "No goddam queer's gonna talk t'me like that!"

"Ed, you'll *kill* him!"

"I said—*let go!*" He flung off Sid and lunged forward again toward Merv who was trying to struggle to his feet.

"Ed!" Sid yelled.

But Ed was already dragging up Merv by the arm again. Merv cried out in fright, then the cry changed to a choking gasp as Ed drove a fist into his stomach. He doubled over with a retching gag but Ed jerked up his head by the hair.

"Apologize!" he said in a voice no longer human. "Apologize, *queer*, or I'll break every bone in your damn body!"

I didn't know what was holding me back until I felt Bob's hand clutching at my shirt. The pounding in my ears fell enough for me to hear him whispering feverishly, "Don't be a *fool!* You can't do any good! He'll just throw *you* out too!"

I think I would have torn loose except that Sid had Ed by the arm again now and was pulling him away from the slumped-over Merv.

"Come on, Ed! For God's sake!"

Ed, not even listening, was talking to Merv in a gutteral, animal-like voice, saying, "You stay away from my camp, ya hear me, ya goddam queer?" You come back here, I'll kill ya. I'll kill ya."

"Come on, Ed." Sid tugging on his beefy arm.

"Not gonna have any damn pervert in *my* camp. Not *my* camp. My job is to take care o' my boys, that's my *job*."

"All right, Ed, all right. He's going. He's going."

We stood there silently until the sound and sight of them had disappeared into the night. Then we moved out to where Merv was sitting on his trunk, bent over, gasping for air.

I remember how the moonlight came out just as we reached him. I remember how he looked up in terror at the sound of our footsteps, I remember the cold light bathing his contorted face, revealing the dark thread of blood dribbling down from his right nostril, the tense parting of his lips around gritted teeth, the almost deranged look in his eyes.

"It's all right, Merv," I said. "It's just us."

He stared at us a long moment, then, as I put my hand on his shoulder, a sob broke in his throat, a sob of wretched, broken will.

"Did you *see* it?" he asked, brokenly. "Did you see what he did to me? The *filthy swine!*"

"Take it easy, Merv," I said. "He's insane."

"Insane." He muttered it after me. "He *is* insane. He should be p-put away."

We helped him up and Bob handed him his glasses which were cracked on the right lens. "You should make him pay for this," Bob said in a thin, strengthless voice.

"He'll pay for it," Merv said, but I don't think he was talking about the glasses. He was still sucking in air fitfully, one hand pressed to his stomach.

"Take it easy, Merv." I said again. "It's all right."

"The swine. The *swine.*" Another sob he couldn't hold.

"Do you have any place to go, Merv?" I asked.

He stood on the moon-white road, his thin chest rising and falling jerkily, his dazed eyes staring at the camp.

"He should be put away," he said in a hollow voice. "The *dirty, filthy-minded—*"

He broke off with a liquid coughing, then closed his eyes and gasped as a spasm of pain struck his stomach. I caught his arm and braced him as he bent over, making pitiful little sounds of pain.

"It's all right, Merv," I said, "all right."

Finally he straightened up, white-faced, breathing heavily.

"All right," he said hoarsely, "I'm all right. Thank you. Thank you."

"Merv, what about it?" I asked. "*Have* you any place to go?"

He stared at me, his lips still trembling. He sniffed to stop the bleeding from his nose.

Then he said, "I'll be all right," and turned away.

I started after him and caught his arm. "Merv, where are you *going?*"

"I'm quite all right, thank you. Leave me alone." His voice was as even as he could make it. "I'll be all right."

"But where are you going?"

"I don't know. Back to the city, I guess. I don't know. I'll be all right. Just leave me alone."

"Merv, maybe Jackie will help you," I heard myself blurting.

He stopped short and glanced over his shoulder. I sensed the questions in his mind. But he didn't ask them. He turned away and started walking again.

"Merv, what about your things?"

He broke stride again, halted. "I'll...well, will you...will you put them somewhere?" he asked. "I...anywhere, anywhere. I'll have someone pick them up. I'll—"

He broke off and started walking quickly up the road, drawing out a handkerchief and dabbing at his nose. Bob came up beside me and we stood there watching him go. I didn't know whether to run after him or not. He sounded as if he knew what he were doing yet, moments before, he'd been sobbing. We watched his long, ungainly form dwindle down the road that ran like a silvered ribbon between the black woods on either side. The black woods of Camp Pleasant.

1.

Breakfast babble sank to a chatter, a hum, then died out completely. I looked up from my scrambled eggs and saw Ed Nolan standing at his table, across his face the expression he wore on occasions of gravity.

"This won't take long," he began. "I'm just gettin' up t'tell ya there's not gonna be any more hikes for a while."

A rumbling of disappointed complaints from the cabins whose hike days were coming up. Big Ed lifted beefy arms.

"Awright, *aw*right," he ordered. "Quiet down." They quieted. "The reason is because the hiking leader quit on us last night."

A surprised buzzing. Scrambled eggs turning to scrambled lead in my stomach. My slapped-down fork made a loud clinking noise in the momentary silence that followed Ed's raised arms but no one seemed to notice it. I pushed my plate away and glanced over at Bob. His face was a mask of unrepressed disgust.

"Him quittin' came as a surprise t'me," claimed Ed Nolan. "But that's the way it goes with jokers like that. Y'can't never trust 'em."

I looked at Sid. His head was bent forward a little and he was staring at his plate.

Big Ed threw on the mantle of good-fellowship.

"Anyway—" he said as though pushing aside all uncharitable thoughts as unworthy of himself—"that's not here or there. When ya run a camp, ya take the good with the bad. So I guessed wrong. Okay. I'm the first one to admit it when I make a mistake. But that's not important. The important thing is I'm here t'look after you boys—" exorbitantly gestured finger—"and that's just what I'm gonna do. Now. I've sent a wire t'the board asking them t'send up a new hike counselor *right away*. In the meantime, though, we'll try t'find someone to take over the hikes soon *as we can. Is that fair enough?*" Magnamimous raising of voice and arms.

"Yeah, Ed." "*Sure*, Ed!" Applause.

In three days, Mick Curlerman was to be assigned to hikes with Sammy Wrazalowsky taking over the Craft Shop. Then, following the Counselor Takeoffs, Sammy Wrazalowsky (fresh from his triumph as the belly-bulging Big Ed) was to be found wanting in managerial know-how and demoted to ring-making again with Bill Beuchre (wood crafts) taking over the shop. No wire was ever sent to the board requesting a new counselor. I learned it from Doc Rainey some time later.

2.

Tony was sitting on the edge of his cot looking at a comic book.

"Howdy, lowlife," I greeted him.

He looked up. "*Hi*-ya, Matt!" That wide, face-halving smile I like so much. "I been waitin'."

"Wait no more," I said. "Let's go."

He grabbed his bat from the cot and got up. "Oh, boy, am I gonna have a game o'ball *t'day!*"

I placed the restraint of a weary hand on his shoulder. I removed the monstrous bat from his hand. "Now, look," I said, "there is to be no ball playing, no lake ducking, no fishing, no hiking, no strenuous activity of any sort until your stitches heal. *You understand me?*"

"Awww, *Matt.*"

"Look," I said, "either you promise me you'll take it easy or you're staying right here in the dispensary. I *mean* it now."

Hangdog expression Number 7-b. "Awww, *Matt.*" A tired, a sadly-patient *Awww Matt.*

"Look, Tony." I lifted his chin with a finger. "You're my friend, aren't you?"

"Sure, Matt, but—"

"Well then. I don't want to see anything more happen to you. Will you promise me you'll do as I say?"

"Aww...."

"For *me*, Tony?"

"Awww...o-*kay.*"

I nudged a friendly fist against his jaw. "Good," I said. "Come on, we'll play some checkers."

"I don't know how."

"I'll teach you."

We returned to our cabin where I taught Tony the intricacies of jumping, kinging and such. I let him win two games and the edges of his grin touched both ears. This lasted about an hour or so. Then Tony read comic books while I worked out a program of easy, almost monotonal songs for Wednesday might's movie intermissions. I padded time as much as possible but then I knew I had to go and gather up the scattered pieces of my glee club to rehearse them for the Sunday service.

"Now, look, Tony," I said, explaining the situation, "I'd like to stay with you but I've got work to do."

"Aw, I don't wanna just stick around here, Matt," he said, having finished all available comic books and lying on his bunk, chafing at invisible bit.

"Well...." I wracked my brain for a solution; which came even though it was a risky one.

"Now, listen to me," I said, sitting on his bunk. "If I let you go to the ball field will you—"

"Oh, boy!"

"Now, *listen!*" He closed his eager mouth. "You've got to promise me you'll just sit on the bench and *watch.*"

"Awww, M—"

"Tony." I put my hand on his shoulder. "Look, if you don't do that, I get into trouble. I'll get bawled out for not taking care of you, don't you see that? I might even lose my job. You wouldn't like that, would you?"

He shook his head. "No, Matt."

"Well then?"

"Okay." He shrugged. "I promise. I'll just watch 'em."

"All right," I said. "I believe you." As I said it, I got the distinct feeling that it might have been the first time in Tony Rocca's young life that anyone said to him—I believe you.

As an indication of purpose, he left his beloved *Louisville Slugger* behind and walked off politely to the ball diamond, wounded hand in pocket. I got together my music and started for the dining hall. It was while I was crossing the log bridge that the tan coupe pulled up in front of the office and braked. Out of it came Jackie dressed in tight denims and a snug black gaucho shirt. I started forward and called him but he didn't hear and went into the office. A sinking sensation crowded my stomach. I trudged across the clearing, bracing myself for what I hoped was not to follow.

As I came up to the screen door of the office, I heard Ed talking to Jackie as he might address a backward child.

"Told him t'take his junk *with* him," said Ed. "Nothin' left around here's far as *I* know."

"But I was *told*," insisted a dulcet-voiced Jackie.

"Sorry, boy. Don't know a thing about it."

"*Well.* I certainly don't understand this."

I stood out by the car until Jackie came out, his face a mild summer storm. When he saw me, he smiled.

"Well, hello there," he said. "Maybe *you* can—"

"Listen," I said hastily, "Merv's things are on the porch of the grocery and drug store up the road."

He looked surprised. "Oh, are you the one who—"

"Look," I said, "I'm in a hurry. Do you know which store I'm talking about?"

"Well, I—"

"As you go up to the road, turn right," I said. "It's just a little ways down the road on the left-hand side."

"Oh." He nodded his head once.

"Where's Merv?" I asked, glancing nervously at the office.

Jackie smacked his lips in disgust. "Gone back to the city. He left on the bus this morning."

"Oh. You know where to go now?"

"Yes. But, tell me...." He twined lax fingers around my arm. "Who *is* that great *oaf* of a man in there?"

"He's our leader," I said and started away from Jackie.

To feel a stiffening of momentary shock as Ed Nolan came out of the office door, his face filled with displeased curiosity.

"What's goin' on here, Harper?" he asked. "What're you talkin' t'*him* for?"

A moment's reprieve saved me as Jackie gunned his motor too much, then geared it badly and started up the slight incline that led to the road. When the noise of the motor had faded, I said that I'd told him where to find Merv's belongings.

"What've *you* got t'do with his belongings?" came the inevitable question.

"We met him on the road last night," I said.

"Who's *we?*"

"Dalrymple and I," I lied on. "We were coming back to camp when we met Loomis."

"What time?" he asked.

"About ten-thirty, I guess." I allowed time for Merv's discovery on the dock, his packing, his beating and then his starting up the road.

"What'd he tell ya?" Ed asked, looking very suspicious.

"Said he was fired," I told him, calmly. "Asked us to put his stuff somewhere for him."

"That's *all* he said?" asked Ed and, for one muscle-tensing moment, I heard that same crawling undertone of irrational violence in his voice.

"That's all," I said. "Why do you ask, Mister Nolan?"

"Never mind that," Ed said grumpily. "What the hell are *you* doin'?"

"Getting ready to rehearse the glee club," I said, feeling a slight measure of enjoyment in the realization that, although Ed despised the very thought of taking boys off a ball diamond and into the world of melody, he couldn't do anything about it short of giving me carte blanche to loaf.

"Oh," he said. "How's it goin'?"

"Fine," I said. "Very good."

"They were kind o' flat last Sunday."

"Oh? I didn't notice." I knew he hadn't either.

"Well...." He looked vaguely disconcerted. "Get on with your work." Turning, he trudged back to the office.

I watched him a moment, then, dumping my music in the dining hall, I began the great trek about camp to gather up the unwilling complement of my club of glee.

It was about an hour later amidst struggles with a wounded and dying *Onward Christian Soldiers* that the screen door of the dining hall wailed open and heavy, sneakered footfalls intruded. I glanced over and saw Big Ed approaching. About the same time, the boys saw him too and, in piecemeal fashion, stopped singing.

There was a vengeful look in Ed Nolan's eyes as he came up to me.

"You were told t'take *care* o' Rocca," was the first thing he said.

A spasm of fear contracted my stomach muscles; not fear of Ed's displeasure but fear for Tony. "What happened?" I asked quickly.

"I found him up at the *ball* field," he said testily. "That how you take care of him?"

"You mean he—"

"He's s'posed t'be in his cabin!"

"Is there anything wrong with him?"

"Anything wrong? Naw, naw, not a thing. He's only got a bandaged foot and a bandaged hand!"

"I don't mean that," I said. "I mean have his stitches opened or anything like—"

"Never mind," said Big Ed.

I realized suddenly that little pitchers with grandiose ears were absorbing the entire scene. "All right," I asided to them, "all of you wait outside till—"

"That's enough *singin'*," Ed immediately countermanded. "Go get some sun and exercise."

"Yay!" A general cheer, a general, floor-shaking exodus around my fuming self.

"I can't very well improve their singing without practice," I said irritably to Ed when the sound of running and screen door slappings had abated.

"Never mind that," he shunted me aside again. "Let's get somethin' clear right now, Harper. You're responsible for your cabin—*twenty-four hours a day!*"

"Mister Nolan, was Tony Rocca playing ball?"

"He probably would've at any second," he answered. "That would've *really* taken care of his hand."

"Mister Nolan," I said, "I knew Tony Rocca was up there. He—"

"You *knew* it!"

"Will you let me finish?" I snapped, catching him flat-footed. "I gave him permission to go up there on the stipulation that he wouldn't do anything besides sit there and watch."

His repressing of anger was plainly visible but he managed it. A look of contempt crossed his features.

"*And you believed him,*" he said.

"*Yes,*" I said, "I believed him. I thought it was time somebody had a little faith in the kid."

"You know *all* about him, don't ya?"

"I know enough," I said, not thinking.

The lines of his face tensed into lines of hard curiosity. "*How* d'ya know?" he demanded suddenly. "Who told ya?"

"Tony," I said.

"Did *Goldberg* tell ya?"

"No. Tony told me." I had to swallow but I didn't.

"I don't like lyin' from my counselors, boy," he said. "If I find out ya been lyin'...."

He left it unfinished, potential. There was silence a moment, each of us staring at the other. Then he turned away, and casually, dropped behind him these words.

"Go help Rocca pack. He's bein' transferred."

"What?" I started forward with a jerky movement. "Transferred? What for?"

He stopped and whirled. "Because you don't know how t'take care of him, that's why!" he stormed.

I shuddered back, thrown off balance by the vehemence of his attack. "That's not true," I said. "It's not true at all."

"I s'pose ya call lettin' him get cut t'*pieces* takin' care of him!"

"These things weren't my fault," I said. "Besides, they're not the important—"

"Aaah, get out o' here!" he snarled. "You're like all of 'em; you so-called brainy boys. All talk and no sense. You're bluffs, *all* o' ya!"

"Sure," I said flatly. "Whose cabin is Tony going to?"

Was that a smile? "MacNeil's" said Big Ed Nolan.

I turned away. "That's *swell*," I said.

Walking back to the cabin, I wondered why Ed hadn't fired me. The only thing I came up with was the fact that he was already short one counselor with Merv ousted. He didn't like me but he couldn't spare me. Not yet.

I found Tony in his bunk, burrowed under the covers, trembling with soundless sobs. I felt tightness fill my chest and throat as I stood by the bunk, looking down at him. Then, with a very tired sigh, I gathered together his things and put them all in his near-empty trunk. Across this I laid his bat like a squire laying down the sword of his slaughtered knight.

I sat down on the mattress beside him. "Tony."

Silence. I put my hand on the shaking lump that was his head. "Tony," I said again, "Pull the cover off your head, Tony. I want to talk to you."

"I ain't *goin'*!"

"Tony, take down the blanket."

"No, I ain't *goin'*!"

Gently, I drew back the covers. His thin cheeks were wet with tears.

"Tony," I said, hoping I'd just imagined the break in my voice.

"Why'd ya *let* 'im?" he asked me pitifully. "Why'd ya *let* 'im, Matt? You *said* I could go t'the ball field."

"I know, Tony," I said. "There was nothing wrong in your going. Mister Nolan just thinks there was."

"Then I don't have t'go?" His thin voice rising hopefully.

I sighed. "I'm afraid so, Tony," I said. "That's what he wants."

He drew in a sob jerkily, his chest shaking with it. "Who's he think *he* is?" he asked. "King *Shit*?"

"Shhh, Tony," I said. "That won't help."

"I *hate* 'im," he said bitterly. "Who's he think he is?"

"Come on, Tony," I said. "I think we'd better get it over with."

"But I *like* this cabin. I know all the fellas in it."

"I know, Tony," I said. "But I can't do anything about it. Really I can't Tony."

"No!" he sobbed, tears pulsing from his eyes again. "I ain't goin'. He can't make me! The dirty son-of-a—"

My finger over his lips cut him short. From the mouths of babes, the phrase occurred ironically.

Then Marty Gingold came in from the dock, dripping lake drops on the floor. He stared at Tony with that brutal frankness of the young. "What'sa matter?" he asked.

"Nothing," I said. I got up and blew out a disgusted breath. "Come on, Tony," I said. "You're only going next door."

"No." Sullen; without hope.

"'S he bein' transferred?" Marty Gingold inquired interestedly.

I nodded curtly. "I'm going next door a second, Tony," I said. "Get your things moved now."

"No."

"Who we gettin'?" asked diplomatic Marty Gingold. "Hope it's someone that can play ball."

"Shut the hell up," said Tony.

"Fungoo," answered Marty.

"Oh...shut up both of you!" I muttered irritably as I went out of the cabin.

I found a disgusted-looking boy flinging clothes into a trunk with furious motions. I glanced at the empty bunk.

"So you're the one," I said. "What's your name?"

"Riley!" He flung the words the way he flung his swim suit into the trunk. "What's *yours?*"

"Mud," I said. He paid no never mind.

"What'sa *matta* with this dump *anyway?*" he asked angrily of the air. "Why the hell do I have t'transfer for some lousy wop!"

"He isn't any happier about it than you are," I said.

"Then what the hell's he *comin'* for?"

"Politics," I said.

"So *what!*" he answered.

That was when I heard the thumping and the bellowing curse from my own cabin. *"Oh...."* With a curse of my own, I lunged out the doorway and bounded to the steps of my cabin.

I found Tony underneath a punching Marty Gingold; a saliva-frothing Tony whose hands were twisted into bone-white claws on Marty's back.

"Bite me, will ya!" yelled Marty Gingold, driving a fist into Tony's head. I dragged his punching pudginess off of Tony.

"What's the matter with you!" I stormed.

"He *bit* me!" accused Marty.

"Son-of-a bitch bastid," Tony said in a low, menacing voice as he got up, "I'll beat ya *brains* out!"

He leaped for Marty and I grabbed him in mid-air, hearing Marty's returned challenge, "You'n what *army!*"

Tony kicked and flailed in my grip, his face twisted with mindless fury. "I'll cutcha heart out!" he screamed at Marty. "I'll cutcha goddam *heart* out!"

"Tony!" My roar echoed off the ceiling and, I guess, deafened him since I shouted it right into his ear.

He looked up at me, breathing hard.

"Tony, stop it," I said. "Stop it. Calm down."

"No kike bastid is gonna—"

"Tony, *shut up!*"

His mouth clamped shut into a living scar.

"You like to be called a *wop?*" I asked angrily. The tensing of his face and body gave me my answer. "Well, Marty doesn't like to be called a kike either."

"He made *fun* o'me," Tony said through gritting teeth.

I looked at him for a solemn moment.

"If he did," I said then, "it's just because he doesn't understand."

Later, I took Tony and his belongings to the new cabin and he never said a word through all of it. He walked beside me and obeyed orders and hung up clothes and made his new bunk. But he never said a word.

3.

Bob and I had been down in the lodge rehearsing a one-act play. We quit about a quarter to nine and Bob went to Ed's cabin to play some cards, I headed for my cabin.

I was about halfway to the ridge on which the senior cabins stood when the sounds reached my ears—scraping shoes, groaning bedsprings and the excited encouragement of boys. I don't know how I knew, I just did, the second I saw that the fight was going on in Mack's cabin. I darted up the rest of the hill and into the cabin. As I entered, I saw Tony on the floor, struggling futiley while another kid—I didn't know him—had his arm around Tony's neck and was squeezing, gasping harshly—"*Surrender? Surrender?*"

Tony could hardly breathe. There was a babbly froth of saliva running across his chin, his lips were drawn back tautly over his teeth. There was blood seeping from beneath the bandage on his wrist and hand. But he wouldn't surrender.

Sitting on a bunk edge, enjoying his ringside seat, was Mack.

"For Christ sake!" I exploded and, bending over, I wrenched the boy's arm from Tony's neck. Immediately there were cries of "*Hey, whattaya doin'!*" and "*Get outta here*, this ain't your cabin."

The boy tried to kick Tony but I shoved him away and he went sailing into two of his buddies, the three of them landing in a heap on the floor. Tony tried to crawl after him, his face still deranged, but I dragged him up by his good arm and held on to him.

"What's the *matter* with you?" I asked Mack, furiously. "You know damn well he's got stitches in his wrist!" I held up Tony's hand. "Look! It's starting to *bleed* again!"

"He started it," Mack said casually. "He wanted t'fight."

"And you let him!"

"None o' my business," said Mack. "If the little wop wants t'fight, it's his business."

"That's fine," I said. "*Great!* You're gonna help him a lot, an *awful* lot."

"Look." Mack got up, the casual look fading from his face. "You run your cabin your way. I'll run mine *my* way."

"Tony's wrist is in bad shape!" I said. "You had no right to let him fight!"

"*Look.*" He came over to me, truculent-faced. "He *asked* for it. Nobody did a thing to 'im."

"I'll *bet*," I said, feeling beneath my finger tips the terrible shaking of Tony's arm.

"Look, you wanna start trouble?" Mack asked.

"Not right now, Mack," I said coldly. "I'll take a rain check on it though."

"You got it, boy," Mack answered. "Any time."

"Come on, Tony," I said.

"I don' wanna," he muttered brokenly, but I don't think he even knew what he was saying.

"Where ya think you're takin' *him*?" asked Mack.

"Out of here," I said.

"Big Ed won't *like* that," he said mockingly.

"Tell him to *sue* me."

I stopped in at my cabin and assigned Charlie Barnett to turn out the lights at nine. Then I put my arm around Tony's shoulders and we started for Sid's tent.

Tony's chest kept twitching with helpless sobs as he trudged along beside me and I felt his flesh trembling under my hand. I tried to ask him some questions but it didn't work; he could hardly talk. All I got was a few shaky, pitiful sounds that made no sense.

We met Sid just as he was coming out of his tent with a flash lantern to make his nightly inspection of the Senior Division.

"What's *up*?" he asked concernedly, seeing us.

"Sid, you've got to get him back to me," I said. "They're gonna eat him alive in Mack's cabin. I found him being choked to death by some little bastard and all Mack was doing was watching. They've probably been on Tony's back all afternoon. *Look* at him for Christ's sake!"

Sid looked. He shook his head restlessly. "Bring him in," he said.

The only one in the tent was Barney Wright who was absorbed in a Spalding catalogue. We put Tony on Sid's cot and Sid wrapped a blanket around his thin shoulders.

"What'sa matter with the kid?" asked Barney.

"He's having it tough in his cabin," Sid answered and, with a vague nod of his gray-haired dome, Barney Wright returned to his baseball illustrations.

We sat on each side of Tony, watching him as he stared at the floor with bleak, hope-lost eyes. Sid tried to talk to him but all Tony could do was shiver and sob. So for a long time there was no sound in the tent but that of Tony and the flutter of turning pages in Barney's catalogue.

Finally though—how well I remember it—Tony reached up and wiped away tears with a grimy fist, sniffing as he did. I held my handkerchief to his nose and he blew into it weakly.

"He's gonna send me away again," he said then, his voice hollow and spiritless.

"Who, Tony?" Sid asked him.

"My pa. He's gonna send me back t'the stir."

"Why, Tony?" I asked.

"'Cause I ain't doin' so good," Tony answered, a single tear appearing in his left eye and running down his cheek. I blotted it away. "He said I'd go back if I didn't do good."

"Tony, no one's going to send you back," I said. "You're all right."

"Naw." Tony shook his head and there was on his face the most helpless expression I've ever seen on a child. "Naw. You don't know 'im. He'll put me in the stir again."

"Why should he?" Sid asked. "You haven't done anything."

"I hit 'im," Tony said, sniffing. "I hit 'im and he don't like that."

I couldn't talk. I just sat there numbly, looking at Tony's thin, despair-ravaged face, hearing him answer Sid's questions.

"Why did you hit him, Tony?"

"'Cause he hit my ma," Tony said. "My ma and me was together when my pa went in the army. My ma worked at night and my Uncle Charlie give us some dough too."

"Didn't your father send money?"

"Yeah but my ma didn't use none of it. She put it in the bank. She made enough dough at night. And my Uncle Charlie give her some dough too."

"What happened when your father came home, Tony?"

"He hit my ma and he hit me. He was always cursin' and gettin' drunk and hittin' us. Ma cried at night. I could hear her, lots."

He shrugged, sniffed.

"And you hit him," Sid said.

"Yeah. He hit my ma in the face and I hit him so he hit me back. Then I went t'the stir." He bit his lower lip to keep back the sobs. "I'm g-goin' back again. He'll make me."

"No, he won't, Tony," Sid told him quietly. "We won't let him."

"Ya can't stop 'im," said Tony defeatedly. "He d-does what he wants t'do."

Later, Sid and I stood over the cot, looking down at Tony as he slept; looking at the tear-streaked cheeks, the light quiver of his thin lips. Then we went out on the porch and sat down on camp chairs, propping our feet on the railing.

"That poor kid," I muttered. "Jesus *Christ*." I shook my head. "He tears my heart out."

Sid shook his head. "He's confused all right," he said.

"What about his story?" I asked.

"I think he believes what he says. But how much does a kid his age know of the facts? All he sees is his old man going away to war. His life is nice while his mother takes care of him. Then his old man comes back and starts beating him. That's all he sees. It all sounds so simple."

He sighed heavily.

"Well, it's not simple; I'd bet money on that. How do we know what happened while Tony's father was away? Christ, for all we know, his mother was sleeping with everybody. *She worked at night*—there's a key phrase for you. And who's this Uncle Charlie? I remember when I was a kid, my dad used to have me call all his friends Uncle—Uncle Bill and Uncle Ned and Uncle Mike." He made a sound that was amused yet not amused. "None of them were related to me. And I'd lay money that Uncle Charlie is no relation of Tony's either."

"And the money in the bank?"

"Maybe Tony's mother *told* him she put it in the bank. But how do we know?"

I stared at the black woods around us, at the occasional pinpoint flare of fireflies.

"It just doesn't figure—the old man going away nice and coming back mean," Sid went on. "There's one point Tony doesn't seem to understand. His old man got custody of him after the divorce. The woman always gets the kid unless she's definitely proved to be unfit."

He exhaled wearily.

"There's one other thing," he said grimly. "All Tony seems to remember is hitting his old man on the back. It's not as simple as that."

There was a long pause and I think I knew what was coming before it came.

"His old man is the one Tony tried to kill," said Sid.

Eyes closing abruptly; shivering. I sat slumped in the canvas chair feeling the cold night wind blowing across my face.

"That's great," I muttered. "That's just great."

It was decided to let Tony sleep on Sid's cot until morning. Sid said it was all right since there was an extra cot in the tent that night anyway. Mel Kramer, the head of the Junior Division being on his day off. Sid also said he'd do whatever he could to get Tony back in my cabin again.

As I walked slowly back to the cabin, I kept thinking about Tony. I thought of how he was going to grow up hard; like a flower transplanted from soft to rocky soil—the beauty gone, only the will to survive left. I might get him back in my cabin but, even then, there was only a little more than a month remaining to the season. In that brief time I might go on wrestling with his several devils, ousting some of them perhaps. But, when the summer ended, he'd go back to his father and, in no time, those devils would return, every damn one of them.

It made me angry. I hated a world where such things could happen to children. Because children were the future. It's a statement made in a million graduation deliveries, it's dull, a cliche. It's true. As I thought that, I sensed something in my mind—like the flare of a torch in deep night. It was something of import, something with a particular meaning for me.

I didn't catch it though. It passed away and was gone and all that was left was the memory of how Tony had looked in sleep—his face pale and drawn, one hand flung across his cheek as if someone were just about to hit him.

4.

During clean-up period, the next morning, Sid came down the line with Tony. I went to the door and looked at them as they approached. Sid saw me and, as they went by, he just shook his head once, slowly. I stood in the doorway watching them go over to Mack's cabin and up the porch steps. A moment's inaudible mumble of conversation, then Sid reappeared.

I met him in front of my cabin. "What did he say?" I asked.

"He wants Tony to stay with Mack."

"You told him about last night?"

"I told him everything," he said. "It just didn't do any good."

"I see."

"Tony will be all right," he said. "I'll keep on Mack's tail and see to it."

I nodded, and Sid left. I went back into the cabin.

A little later when morning activity began, I met Mack as he was starting for the athletic fields.

"What're you doin' here?" he asked, trying to look surprised.

"What are you talking about?" I asked.

"This is your day off."

"No, it isn't," I said.

He shrugged. "Oh, I thought it was."

I went to the dining hall and started helping Bob with play rehearsals. About eleven-fifteen, I left the dining hall to go for a swim and met Big Ed. I braced myself for a discussion about Tony but all he said was, "What're *you* doin' here?"

"What do you mean?" I asked.

"This is your day off," he said.

"No, it isn't," I told him. "Next Thursday is."

"Didn't MacNeil tell ya?"

"Tell me what?"

"He changed days with ya. You're off today."

"*What?*" I stared at him. "Nobody told *me* anything about it."

Big Ed looked as bland as his feeble acting powers would allow.

"S'not my fault," he said, shrugging. "MacNeil said you wouldn't mind. Said he asked ya."

"Well, he *didn't*. Why should I change with him?"

"If it wasn't down on the schedule already," said Big Ed, "I could change it back, but it's too late now."

I looked very obvious daggers at him.

"What's the difference?" he said carelessly. "One day's as good as another."

"Sure," I said.

"You might as well take off," he said, turning away. "You missed a couple hours already." He started for the office, saying over his shoulder, "Oh, and...forget about Rocca. You don't have t'worry about him

86

any more." He left me with that and the office screen door slapped shut behind him.

I took a shower and shave, even dressed; then realized there was no place to go and I had no desire to look for one. With a curse, I lay down on my bunk. I sat up and started to write a letter. This failed. In the middle of the first paragraph, I scratched out everything and flung the crumpled sheet across the cabin. Next I tried reading but that didn't work either. I finally fell into a restless semi-doze. When the dinner horn sounded I went out and stood on the hill crest looking at the gray, shifting lake. A moment was profitably employed in visions of holding the heads of Ed and Mack beneath that cold-looking surface. This, too, passed.

I started walking. I wasn't hungry so I by-passed the talk-buzzing dining hall. I wasn't sick so I went by the dispensary. I wasn't a section leader so I avoided their tent; and I wasn't Jack Stauffer so I stayed out of his cabin.

Nolan's cabin was silent and dim as I opened the kitchen screen door and entered. I moved into the living room and saw that the bedroom door was closed.

I settled myself on the couch and began reading about Joan Collins. Then I dropped the magazine and tried to penetrate the prose forests and off-center cuteness of *The New Yorker*, gleaning only one mild laugh from the cartoons. Finally I tossed aside the tenth *Life* magazine and looked around the room with unamused eyes.

I got up and walked over to the phonograph. I looked through the stack of popular records without interest, then found the classical albums on a shelf below the player. I picked out the Pathetique as being a composition fitting my frame of mind and warmed up the tuner. The music started and I sank down on the couch again to stare at the hoop rug and listen.

The main theme of the first movement was just receiving its first presentation by the strings when the bedroom door was unlocked and opened abruptly.

Ellen stood there looking at me. She was wearing only a slip.

"Where's Ed?" she asked.

"I don't know," I said.

"What're *you* doing here?" she asked.

"It's my day off," I said.

She said nothing. She slumped a little, then straightened.

"What're you doing here?" she asked again but this time I didn't answer. I looked curiously at her, noting her tangled hair.

"Why're you playing my music?" she asked in a sullen voice. "Who gave you permission?"

"Nobody. I just—"

She started for the record player. "*My* music," she said. "Who gave you the permission?"

There was a little break in her voice as she spiked the last sentence. I got up nervously, still staring at her. She stood leaning against the case the record player was on. Then she replaced the record arm and the music started again.

"S'all right," she said. "It's all right for you to listen. You like music. You can listen because you like it. You do like it? Don't you? You said you—"

"Yes," I said, "I like it."

"You listen to it," she said. "He doesn't like music. He *hates* music."

She turned back to me suddenly and her chest jerked convulsively as she hiccupped. Something pulled in my stomach muscles, then dropped them. I gaped at her.

"That's right," she said, "I'm drunk. I'm awful drunk."

"*Ellen.*"

"What's the matter, haven't you ever seen anybody drunk before?" No answer from me.

"You think I'm terrible, don't you?" she asked. "You think I'm no good."

I shook my head, speechless.

"*Don't look at me like that!*"

"Ellen."

"Damn you!" She started toward me suddenly. "I said don't look at me like—"

Her foot slipped on the hook rug and, with a gasping cry, she started to fall. I jumped forward and caught her, feeling her fingers clutch my shoulders again, feeling her body against me, soft and clinging; her voice suddenly different.

"Matt, don't," she said.

I put her down on the couch nervously and stood beside it. I felt as if someone was trying to crush my heart with a mail-gloved hand.

"Don't hate me, Matt," she said. "Please. I can't help it. I don't do it to be mean."

"I'd better go, Ellen."

"Don't go," she begged.

I sat down beside her, hearing the Pathetique symphony playing as if from another world. She put her shaking hand on mine.

"Do you think I'm awful, Matt?" she asked, her breath clouding over me.

"You're not awful," I said. "You're afraid. You're unhappy."

For a moment I thought of Ed coming back and finding Ellen like this but the idea faded in my concern for her. She looked so pitiful and lost; like a little girl deserted by everyone. Her hand kept stroking at mine helplessly. She didn't seem to notice the slip strap falling off her shoulder. She didn't seem to notice anything in her desire to explain. I sat there, numbly, listening.

"Do you hate me, Matt?" she asked. I shook my head. "You shouldn't be here. It's not right you should—"

She pulled back her hand, her face hardening.

"Why am I talking to you?" she asked. "This's *my* house. *Mine.*"

"Of course it—"

"Oh, stop talking to me!"

Her head slumped forward, she stared at her hands, then ran the shaking fingers through her hair. "Go away," she muttered. "Leave me alone."

"Ellen, why—?"

"I'm nothing," she said. "I'm nobody. Don't worry about me."

"Ellen, why did you marry him?"

I couldn't help asking the question I'd asked myself a hundred times.

She looked up at me quickly. "Why shouldn't I marry him!" she asked. "You want me to stay single all my life?"

I said nothing. I just stared at a young woman I couldn't understand but couldn't leave.

"You want to know?" she asked. "All right, I'll tell you, you're so damn curious."

She drew in a rasping breath.

"They wanted to get rid of me," she said. "They...j-j-just got tired of having me around the house, tired of me eating their food, tired of me using up their damn precious money! So they *sold* me! That's what it amounts to. *Why don't you marry Mister Nolan, dear?* He's a good man and very attentive. I'm sure he loves you very much."

Her head fell forward again.

"I'm sure he loves you very much," she repeated in a low, hollow voice.

"It's all right," I said without thinking.

She looked at me with a thin smile I took for contempt although it was more than that.

"All right," she repeated my words. "What do you know? *All right*." Another shaking breath. "If you knew," she said. "If you only knew...."

She shook her head. "No," she said. "No, I wouldn't tell you. I wouldn't shock you."

"That's not why you won't tell me" I said.

She drew back with dizzy hauteur. "Don't talk to me like that," she said.

Abruptly, she sobbed and flung a hand across her eyes. "Don't talk to me like that!" she said. "Leave me alone!"

"No." I couldn't help it. I put my hand on her shoulder. She twisted away.

"Don't touch me!"

"Ellen, I'm not—"

She drew back with a frightened look, biting on one finger. Then she drew the finger away and, visibly, tried to pull herself together. She drew up the shoulder strap suddenly and tugged the slip bodice up over the white tops of her breasts.

"You'd better go," she said heavily. "This is no place for you. You— you'll be corrupted, you'll get sick at what you see. I don't want to—"

She stopped as I put my hand on hers, tightly.

"I'm not sick," I said.

"I'm warning you," she told me. "Go away."

"No."

She looked at me, a dozen different emotions moving through her eyes. "But you—" she started, and that was all. It happened.

If I'd read it in a book, I'd have laughed at it. If I'd seen it in a movie, I'd have scoffed and not believed. Yet, I swear it was as if a power beyond us threw us together. No externals caused it. The room was dim and unattractive, the air chilly. Neither of us was looking very good at the moment. Even the music had stopped.

Only the scratching of the needle provided the background of our irrevocable kiss.

In that moment, her hands clutched at my back and I could feel her nails, slowly raking. I ran my hands over her warm shoulders and back. I felt her soft, moist mouth crushed against mine and I couldn't have stopped if Ed Nolan had walked into the room with a loaded gun. It wasn't a kiss; it was a mindless and despairing hunger. *Julia!* my mind cried even though I knew that Julia was dead.

Once I saw a woman on a curb watching a truck hit her little boy. I saw that look on Ellen's face.

"Oh, no," she begged someone, anyone. "Oh, no—no. Dear God, no." She shoved back from me, looking horrified.

"Ellen."

"Leave me alone. Oh, please. *Please.*"

I pushed up quickly, all of it flooding over me—Ellen, Ed, the absolute impossibility of it. I backed away, her terrified eyes on me.

"It never happened," she said. "It never happened. Do you hear me?"

"It happened." It was all I could say.

"No!" Her lips twisted back in anguish. "It *didn't!*"

I started toward her but she jerked back with such a throat-wrenching sob that I suddenly realized it had to stop right then or it would never stop.

As the kitchen door slammed shut behind me, I could still hear her shuttered sobbing—if only in my mind. I walked dazedly along the path, hardly noticing the drizzle. My face felt as if it was on fire, my body shuddered without control. I kept swallowing something that wouldn't go down. All I could think of was that I couldn't stand to see anyone. I left the path and walked through the wind-rustled woods until I'd reached the road. Then, ignoring the mist-like rain in my face, I walked to *The Crossroads Tavern.*

It took an hour and three drinks to stop my hands from shaking.

FOUR

1.

I found Tony cleaning garbage cans that morning. He was sitting in front of the kitchen door, scrubbing way inside a deep garbage can with his bad hand.

"What the—?"

Tony looked up, his face a mask of hate; which softened only a trifle when he saw me.

"What's he making you clean garbage cans for?" I asked.

"Because he's a *bastard*," Tony said bitterly.

"Did you have a fight?"

"So—I had a fight."

"Oh, *Tony*. Who with? Oh, never mind—what's the difference? Tony, when are you going to stop fighting?"

"When they stop pickin' on me," he said: the story of his life.

I looked at him a moment, then noticed that there was blood seeping from under the edges of his bandage.

"How long has it been bleeding?" I asked.

"What do *I* care?" he snapped.

"Can't you clean the can with your other hand?"

"I'm a *lefty*."

Another moment of me returning his truculent gaze. Then I reached out and put my hand on his shoulder. He pulled away.

"Come on, Tony," I said quietly. "I'm on your side; you know that."

"Nobody's on my side."

"Tony."

"Well...none o' ya *do* nothin'!" he said angrily. "Ya all shit in ya pants when that fat slob comes around!"

"Wait a minute," I said, turning away abruptly.

"Sure!" he said. "I got *plenty* o'time! I'll be here all day!" I heard him fling his wooden brush into the can.

※　※　※

Ed Nolan looked up from his desk. "Whatta *you* want?" he inquired.

"Tony Rocca can't clean those cans any more."

"What business is it of yours?"

"His hand is bleeding. He can't clean garbage cans in that condition."

"I seem t'remember takin' him out of your cabin," said Big Ed.

"Whether he's in my cabin or not does not alter the fact that his hand is bleeding. His stitches have probably—"

"I told ya he's not your concern any more," he said, his voice rising.

"You mean you're going to let him—"

"And I told you to stay out o' my way," he snapped.

"All right," I said. "*All right.*" I walked down along the lake edge until I reached Doc Rainey's tent. I told him about Tony and his face grew worried. He put down his fountain pen and blew out a long, tired breath.

"You can stop it, can't you?" I asked.

"I'm afraid not, Harper. I—"

"For Christ's sake, isn't there *any* stop to his abuses?"

"Is it really as bad as all that?" Doc asked me. "Don't you think Ed would stop the boy if he thought he wasn't well?"

"No," I said, "I don't think it."

"Now, son," he said, "aren't you being carried away a little?"

"All right," I said, "I'm being carried away." I turned for the tent entrance. "But I'm going to get that kid off that damn detail if I get thrown out of camp for it. I've had it."

"Son, don't do anything you'll be—"

When he didn't finish I looked back and saw that he was rising from the table.

"All right," he said wearily, "I'll see what I can do."

I stopped off at the dispensary as Doc headed for the dining hall. Ten minutes later, Miss Leiber and I came up to where Ed and Doc were looking at Tony's hand.

"He's all right," I heard Ed say. "It's just a little—" He broke off suddenly and glared at me as we came up. I avoided his small eyes as Miss Leiber plucked up Tony's hand and examined it.

"Well," she said in a disgusted voice, "This boy will have to come back to the dispensary again."

"Why?" Ed asked.

"Why?" she said. I had to restrain a grin at the way she spoke to him. "The boy's stitches have opened, that's why. *Cleaning garbage cans*! *Uh!*"

"You sure?" Ed's voice was sullen.

Miss Leiber didn't answer but, with a hiss, she grabbed Tony's good hand and said, "*Come on.*"

"Don' wanna," Tony said.

"Would you prefer *bleeding* to death!" she asked, half-dragging him off.

When I turned back, Ed Nolan was looking at me with an expression that made me glad Doc was there.

"So," Ed said. "I guess ya think ya beat me."

"Beat you?" I said as blandly as possible. "I wasn't trying to beat anybody. I was only concerned with—"

"I'm not *interested* in what you have t'say," Ed interrupted. He reached out his right arm and poked my chest with a sausage finger. "As of now, *boy*," he said, "You're on my shit list. Before the summer's over, you'll wish ya'd never *heard* o' this camp."

"We'll see," I said.

He tensed suddenly and I tensed with him, expecting the worst. Then, with what must have been a superhuman effort on his part, he forced down the anger and managed a twisted smile.

"Go ahead," he said. "Be cute. Be as cute as ya like. You'll be crawlin' before I'm done with ya. You'll be *beggin'* me t'fire ya."

"Take it easy, Ed," Doc said. "Harper was only trying to—"

"Keep out o' this, Doc," Ed said. "This isn't your business."

"I run this camp *too*, Ed," Doc said, suddenly cold.

Ed glanced at him, looking blank. "Awright, Doc," he said. "Take it easy. I didn't mean nothin' against you. It's this jaybird I got my eye on." Finger pointing at me again.

"*Good luck*," I told him.

2.

When I entered the Nolan cabin that night, Mack, Ed and two other counselors were playing poker at a card table, Bob was sitting in a wicker chair reading a book, Ellen was on the couch, looking at a *Life* magazine. I sat down beside her.

"How have you been?" I asked.

"Fine," she murmured.

"Good," I said, then looked over at Bob. "What are you reading?" I asked.

He held up the book. "I can't see it," I said loudly.

"*Passage to India*," he said.

"That's a good book," I said. "I read it twice."

"I don't care if ya read it ten times, Harper," Ed cut in. "Pipe down if ya want t'stay here."

"Sure, Ed," I said. "Sure, I'll pipe down."

I looked back at Ellen. "You look very pretty tonight," I said.

Her smile was more flustered than pleased. "Thank you," she managed. I nodded, glancing at Ed who was just lowering wary eyes.

"That a new dress?"

"What? Why...why no, I've—"

"You heard what I said, Harper," Ed Nolan said.

"Yes, sir," I said. "Yes, I did."

"Shut up then or clear out."

"Sure, Ed," I said. "Sure. I'll shut up." I looked at Bob. "Chess, Bob?" I asked.

He smiled nervously. "Okay," he said softly.

"Excuse me, Ellen," I said.

She didn't answer but, for a moment, our eyes held and I got the feeling that she understood.

Bob and I set up the board on the other card table. As I put my men on the squares, I kept glancing at Mack. Abruptly I swept half my pieces off the board onto the floor and saw the poker players start out of their rapt concentration. Ed's head snapped around and he glared at me.

"Butter fingers," I said.

I made the first move without thought, then rested my chin on my palms and stared at Mack. From the corners of my eyes, I noticed Ellen looking at me and I glanced over and smiled. Her lips seemed to stir but she said nothing.

Then I stared at Mack again. After a few moments he glanced over. "Whattaya *lookin'* at?" he asked.

"Nothing," I said, and he went back to his cards. I kept staring at him.

"Your move," Bob said.

"My move?" I said loudly.

"Listen, boy—" Ed started angrily, and I made a face of much concern.

"Oh...*gee*, Ed, I'm sorry. I forgot myself."

I made another thoughtless move and stared at Mack again. Mack glanced over at me, growing suspicious.

"You lookin' at me?" he asked.

I shook my head, a sincere expression of negation on my face. Then I saw him lean over and whisper something to Ed and Ed looked up at me, a contemptuous curl to his lips. I knew exactly what they were talking about.

"How come you're not in your cabin, boy?" Ed asked me.

"My cabin?" I asked. "Why should I be in my cabin, Ed?"

"Thought ya might want t'tell your boys some stories," said Ed, winking at Mack. Mack snickered.

"No, I'm not as good as Merv was," I said. I could feel Bob looking at me.

"I bet you're not," Ed said, hopelessly unbland. "Loomis was good at lots o' things, wasn't he?"

"*Yes*. He was. That's because he was so intelligent."

Ed and Mack exchanged a man-of-the-world look. "That's because he was so intelligent," said Ed to Mack.

"Oh, is that why?" Mack said. "I thought it was somethin' else." They both chuckled.

"No," I said. "It was because he was so intelligent. What did *you* think it was?"

"Not a thing," said Mack, exchanging a grin with Ed. "Not a thing." Snicker. "*Dear boy.*"

"Oh," I said. Loudly. "*I* see. I thought maybe you had something intelligent to offer the conversation."

Even Mack couldn't miss that. I sat looking at his glowing face, thinking about the rain check.

"You lookin' for trouble?" Arthur MacNeil asked me.

"Who, me?" I said. "No, not me. I never look for trouble. I like peace and quiet."

"I thought ya would," Mack said scornfully.

"Would *what*, Mack?"

"Wouldn't want no trouble." He glanced aside to a pleased Ed Nolan.

"Trouble, Mack?" I said, my voice getting harder. "That's my middle name, Mack. Didn't you know that?" I stared into the eyes of Arthur MacNeil without blinking.

He put down his cards.

"I think you're all bull," he said. "What d'ya think o' that?"

"*Ed.*" Ellen's voice was faint, lost in the shuffle.

"I don't think anything of it," I said. "It isn't worth thinking about. Have you got something in your files that's *worth* thinking about?"

"Ya wanna step outside!" Mack flared.

"Now that's worth thinking about," I said.

"Listen, you—"

"Awright, *hold* it!" Ed ordered. He looked over at me. "Are ya just blowin' off gas as usual, boy, or have ya got the guts t'back up all your noise?"

"No, I have no guts," I said. "I'm scared to death. I'm quaking in my boots. All of us fellas who have an I.Q. of over *forty* always quake in our boots at the thought of a fight."

"I thought s—" he stared, then figured it out. Red splotches moved up his cheeks and he stood up suddenly. "Maybe y'don't wanna fight, Harper," he said, "but you're gonna."

"*Ed.*" Ellen unheard.

"Is that right?" I said. "Who do you have in mind, Ed?"

Mack was standing now beside Ed.

"Get your ass off that chair, Harper," Ed said furiously, "and get outside."

"Ed, *please!*" Ellen said.

"That's enough, El," Ed told her. He gestured with his head toward the kitchen. "Go on. *Get!* You're gonna *fight!*"

"Fight!" I said. "Fight! The very thought appalls me. We fellas who read books never fight! We fellas who like good music and have a vocabulary of more than twenty words are scared to *death* of fighting! We fellas who can conceive of anything in the world that isn't brutish and ignorant and vicious and cruel!" A deep, shuddering breath emptied my lungs. "We never fight," I said, "except—" I glared at Mack—"Maybe once in a while." I flung off Ed's arm. "*Let go,*" I said in a low voice, "I'm fighting him. You don't have to escort me."

"Ed, *stop* it," Ellen begged, following. "You can't let—"

"Stay *out* o' this, El," Ed demanded. "This jaybird's been askin' for it a long time. Now he finally talked himself into it."

"Looks like it," I said. "Sure looks like it." I wasn't feeling quite as flippant as I sounded. I took off my jacket. "Hold this, will you?" I asked Ed. He showed teeth. "Oh," I said, "I thought you'd like to hold it." I tossed it to a tight-faced Bob, then turned back to Mack.

"All right, Mack," I said, "let's get into high gear."

He let go with a haymaker that would have ended the whole thing one-two-three if I hadn't leaned back, fast. The impetus of his swing sent him flailing to one side and down on one knee.

"Good show," I said. "That's what I like about you, Mack. You know exactly what you're doing."

Mack lunged at me again, his right fist driving into my left shoulder. I staggered to one side and drove a right into his face which grazed his cheek. He fell back a little, then dove in again. We clinched and I saw the glaring bulb over the kitchen doorway spinning around us as we ripped and stumbled over the uneven ground. I could feel the hard blocks of muscles in Mack's arms too and I realized, with not a little shock, that he was probably three times as strong as I was.

Abruptly, his right hand was free and he drove it at my stomach. My flung-down left arm deflected his hard fist a little but it drove into the flesh over my left hip, sending a knife of pain into my guts. I sucked in air through gritted teeth and managed to knock aside the left he was throwing at my face. I could feel the wind of it.

Before he could recover, I drove another right into his face and got me a rewarding splash of blood from both nostrils. "Son-of-a-bitch!" he snarled, leaping at me again. I jumped to the side, gasping at the pain under my heart. "Temper, temper, Mack," I managed. "You mustn't—"

He caught me on the chest with a miscalculated blow at my head and I fell back toward the tree that stood before the kitchen window. In a flash of side vision, I saw Ed Nolan's face, twisted into a mask of vicious exultance. It gave me back the strengthening anger I needed to regain balance as Mack rushed in again.

I knocked aside his right but it was so strongly driven that it still grazed the side of my head. I threw a right at his stomach but hit his belt buckle instead. I felt his left driving into my right arm, numbing it and, with a lunge, I rammed my left into his face again, putting my body behind it. More blood.

"*Son*-of-a!" he gasped, wiping the blood away furiously.

I should have taken advantage of his pause but I stood there, breathing heavily, until he caught his breath and advanced on me again, slowly now.

"That last one was for Merv," I said, wondering why I was trying to make him angrier than he already was. "The one on the nose, I mean."

"Queer!" he snarled, swinging at me.

I jumped in so close that his wrist banged against my shoulder. Then I drove a hard left into his chest and a right to his jaw. A flash of terrible pain ran up my right arm as I hit his rock-like jaw. I tried not to show it. Mack staggered back.

"Queer?" I gasped, grateful for the temper he was recalling. I drove a furious, body-weighted right into his face and couldn't help the groan as fiery pain flew up my arm again. With a furious sob, Mack drove his right into my stomach and that was almost that. I doubled over with a gasp, then felt something like a mallet blow on my head and went reeling back into the tree, getting my breath knocked out.

"*Finish* 'im!" Ed cried suddenly and, once more, gave me the strength to get up.

Three Macks came running out of the wavering night and one of them hit me—hard. I went flinging back against the tree again, banging my head against the trunk.

"*Stop* it!" Ellen screamed but no one did.

Mack drove a fist into my stomach again but I doubled over so fast he missed with his next punch at my head. I felt him stumble heavily, off balance, against me and, straightening up I accidentally drove the top of my skull against his jaw. I don't know what he felt but, for me, it was like getting hit with a shillelagh.

Mack staggered back, one hand to his face. I took a feeble swing at one of him but it was the wrong one. He lurched forward and hit me in the face. I put what I had left into a left to his stomach and, this time, got a sucked-in breath for my efforts.

"*Bastid!*" Mack gasped.

"Get 'im!" roared Ed. "*Get* 'im!"

Mack swung and missed as I ducked and I hit him weakly in the nose again. He cried out in furious pain, then, with a lunge, threw himself against me, pinning me to the tree and pummeling at my body. It felt like someone beating me with a log. I started slumping.

I don't know when it was he drew back a little to get a final ending haymaker at my jaw. It seemed like days. All I know is that I could see it coming and sensed that either I got out of the way or it was all over. So, as it came, I fell heavily to one knee and jerked in my head.

Mack's cry of agony was awful as, swinging with all his might, he hit the tree instead of my face.

I fell back limply against the trunk and, through a mist, saw him stumble back, crying hoarsely, "My *wrist*, my *wrist*!"

"Come 'ere, boy," Ed ordered suddenly, rushing to him

Everything was silent then except for Mack's teeth-clenched whines.

"Uh-oh," I heard Ed say. "Let's get t'the dispensary."

I watched dizzily as he led the whimpering Mack up the path. I tried to struggle up but fell back weakly against the tree. Legs appeared beside me, then a blurred face and I felt a hand slide under my armpit.

"Come on, Matt," Bob said. "Upsy daisy."

"Uzzy daizy," I muttered, groggily, pushing to one knee. "*Oh!*" I doubled over sharply, hands clutched over my stomach as pain exploded therein. I opened my mouth, gagging. Then, after a few seconds, I closed it and gasped for breath as I realized I wasn't going to lose my supper after all. I felt cold night wind on my sweat-dewed forehead as Bob helped me to straighten up on wobbly legs. I blinked and shook my head a little, clearing things up in time to see the other two counselors leaving.

"Bring him inside, Bob," I heard Ellen say then and I looked over to where she wavered in the kitchen doorway.

"I'm all right," I said.

"Come on, Matt."

I walked unsteadily through the kitchen and into the living room with Bob's hand under my elbow. Ellen disappeared into the hall and I heard the light flick on as Bob put me down on the couch.

"Oh," I said and grimaced at the stomach pain. "Oh."

Bob looked worried. "You all right, Matt?" he asked.

I shook my head dizzily. "Sure," I said. "Sure. For a guy that got killed."

"You didn't get killed," he said. "You put him in his place."

"Huh," I grunted. "He killed me."

"No, he didn't," he said and, by God, if he didn't sound as proud as if we'd both been fighting Mack. "He'll never bother you again."

Ellen came in then with a first-aid box, looking very pale and drawn. She sat down beside me on the couch.

"How do you feel, Matt?" she asked gently, looking at me concernedly.

"How do I look?" I asked, smiling weakly.

"*Wonderful.*" It came out before she could stop it and, even though it was barely a whisper, I knew Bob had heard it.

"Am I cut?" I asked as she opened the first-aid box.

She swallowed, then forced a smile. "A little," she said. "On your forehead."

"What happened to Mack?"

She shook her head.

"I think he broke his wrist," I heard Bob say.

"Oh. I'm sorry."

Ellen started dabbing at my forehead with alcohol-soaked cotton and I winced as a thin streak of fire ignited there. Her face twitched and she bit her lower lip.

"It's all right," I said. "Burn away, doctor."

I looked into her eyes but she averted them.

"That's a nice dress," I said. She smiled faintly, her eyes starting to glisten.

I couldn't help it. I put my hand out and closed the fingers spasmodically over her left arm. I felt how her flesh trembled under my touch.

"Ellen," I said.

She looked as if she were about to cry.

"Bob," I said quickly, not looking at him, "would you check my cabin and see if Sammy's all right?" Sammy Wrazolowsky was subbing for me until eleven.

"But—"

I looked up quickly at him and he swallowed, glancing at Ellen. "All right," he said quietly. "All right, Matt. You...want me to come back and help you to—"

"No, I'll be all right," I told him.

My heartbeat was a slow timpani as he turned and headed across the room. When the screen door slapped shut, I turned back to her. She was staring at her hands.

"Ellen," I said.

She bit her lips and tears started to her eyes. "No, Matt," she said. "No. You're wrong. I'm only concerned with your—health."

"That's not true," I said.

She raised her eyes to me, shimmering with tears.

"Don't," she said. "Oh, *please* don't, Matt."

"Are you so afraid of it?" I asked.

"Yes," she said. "More than you can ever know."

I looked at her in silence a moment. Then I said, "I love you, Ellen."

"*No.*"

"Why not?"

She stared at me blankly for a long while. For a moment, I thought she was going to throw herself against me, then she shuddered and drew back.

"No," she said. "You don't really, Matt. You're just trying to be sweet. You haven't thought it out at all. I know you don't—love me."

"How do you know?" I asked.

She only shook her head.

"Ellen, how do you know?"

"Because, we haven't known each other long enough," she said.

"Because you don't know anything about me. Because—you just can't."

I wanted so desperately to pull her against me and tell her she was wrong. But something in me kept me from it; something in me that knew she was speaking the truth. She must have seen it on my face for it seemed to provide her with the withdrawal she needed. Her hand reached out and stroked my cheek.

"You're very sweet, Matt," she said. "And I appreciate your—your flattery."

"Is that all?" I said.

"That's all there can be," she said, but that look was in her eyes again, even worse. "No matter what I—what you think you feel," she amended hastily. "Believe me, it's—"

She tried to throw it off. She dabbed at my forehead again, a smile faltering on her lips.

"You are very brave," she said. "Mack is very strong." She swallowed. "And...I liked what you said," she went on. "I was very—"

I leaned over and kissed her warm mouth. She remained motionless, neither resisting nor accepting. As I drew back my head, she smiled at me and kept it all hidden except for her eyes.

"If things were otherwise," she said quietly, "I might love you but—" The smile faded. "Well," she said, "You need someone better." It hurt her but she said it.

"Oh, stop it," I said, not knowing whether I felt sympathy or anger. "There's nothing wrong with you but unhappiness."

All she did was shake her head slowly. I put my hands on her shoulders and tried to draw her to me but she held back.

"No, please," she asked. "That just makes us forget the truth." She looked at me pleadingly. "No more, Matt. *Please*. If it will make you happy—yes, I love you. But—" Her small hands held me away. "That's not enough, Matt; you know it isn't enough. There are too many things against us. You know it as well as I."

The rest was leftovers—her bandaging my forehead, getting me a drink of water. It was as if everything had been said and we were strangers again. Love? It was out of the question even though I sensed that she wanted me to tell her otherwise. But I couldn't tell her. I wasn't sure enough.

On the way back to the cabin, I saw a light in the dispensary and saw Miss Leiber washing up inside.

"Miss Leiber?"

She started and whirled. "Who's that?" she asked in a frightened voice.

"Matt Harper," I said.

"You scared me half to death," she said irritably.

"I'm sorry. Where's MacNeil?"

"Being driven to a hospital."

"Oh. Broken wrist?"

"At least," she said. She squinted suspiciously at the screen door. "Were you the one he was fighting?"

I swallowed. "Yes," I said.

She shook her head in disgust. "Fighting, fighting, fighting," she said. "Is that all you young men do?"

"No," I said. "Sometimes we love." She looked at me with eyes that did not understand.

3.

The argument between Ed and Doc Rainey came three days latter.

Lights were out, the kids were, presumably, out and I was in the dining hall getting some music I'd left on the piano earlier that day. I was on my way out with the music when the outside office door banged shut and a bar of light threw itself through the inner doorway that led to the dining hall.

"No use talkin' about it, Doc," I heard Ed Nolan say. "We're gonna do it and that's all there is to it."

"Ed, for God's sake, use your head," Doc said in a voice that was, for him, agitated. "You'll be cutting your own throat, can't you see that? Don't you think the boys will tell their parents about it?"

"So what if they do?" Ed asked stubbornly.

"Ed, you know good and well what happened last time."

I moved across the floor quietly.

"At least eliminate the Junior Division," Doc said. "For God's sake, you can't expose a seven-year-old boy to things like that."

"Never too young," said Ed, still obdurant. "Christ, you'd think it was somethin' awful. It's fun, Doc, *fun*."

A tense silence, then Doc saying, "All right, Ed, but just remember this'll have to be your responsibility. I can't back you on this one. If there's any—"

"Nobody's askin' you to back me," Ed told him. "It's my show."

I heard a drawer opening and shutting, then the squeak of a heavy body sinking into a chair.

"You're making a mistake, Ed," Doc said.

"Then I'll make it, goddam it!" Ed said angrily. "It's my camp and I'll do what I please with it!"

"You're not going to have it long doing things like this," said Doc.

"I guess that'll really break your heart, won't it, Doc?" Ed said contemptuously. "If I get the bounce, that'll really disturb ya." His voice stiffened. "You've had your eye on Pleasant since I *been* here. Ya never *did* get over them puttin' me over you—even though ya been here two years more than me. Have ya?"

"You're just trying to start an argument, Ed," Doc told him. "I'm not going to—"

"Ya *can't* argue with me, that's why!" Ed interrupted, lashing out angrily. "Ya know damn well ya been doin' a slow burn ever since they give me the camp over your head. Ya been just waitin' t'see me get the boot," Ed said. "Just *waitin'*."

"Is that why I'm trying to talk you out of this Madame La Toure business?" Doc asked.

"Never mind," Ed said.

"Your logic is bad, Ed," Doc said. "If I'd wanted to see you 'get the boot' as you put it, all I'd have had to do was sit back and let you cut your own throat. I didn't have to keep pleading with you year after year to keep you from doing a hundred and one things that would have ended your directorship. All I'd have had to do was sit back and watch you make a noose and hang yourself with it."

"You through?" Ed said.

"Just about," Doc said. "Just about. I'm through trying. After tonight you can do as you damn well please."

"I always have done as I damn well please!" Ed stormed. "You tryin' t'tell me that—"

"No point in trying to tell you anything, Ed!" Doc shouted back. "That's futile business. You get what you want. You wanted Loomis out so you saw to it that he *got* out."

I felt myself stiffen.

"Loomis got *himself* out!" Ed yelled. "I didn't do a thing! I s'pose you'd've told me t'keep 'im in camp until he raped some kid!"

"Loomis was a perfectly honorable young—"

"Honorable, crap!" Ed said loudly. "He was a *queer*!"

"All right, Ed," Doc said, his voice suddenly tired. "All right. I wash my hands of it. Have your fool show. I won't say another word."

"Wouldn't matter if ya *did*!"

Doc's laugh was brief; a sort of tragically accepting laugh.

"You always have to have the last word, don't you?" he said. Then, for a moment, his voice grew hard. "Want the camp? Yes, I want it, I've always wanted it! And with the damn fool way you're running it—I'll have it too!"

After that, Doc left. I did too; returning to my cabin where I undressed, got into pajamas and bathrobe and went up to Paradise. Then I started back.

I was just going by Mack's cabin when I heard the door open halfway and saw one of the kids standing there.

"Psst," he said. "*Hey*," his voice hushed and timorous.

I stopped and went over, shining my light on his face a second to see who it was. It was one of the boys I didn't know.

"What is it?" I asked.

"Mack's sick," he said. "He's makin' funny noises."

I went up the warped steps and into the darkened cabin. "What's up?" I heard a voice ask from one of the dark bunks. "Go to sleep," I said and went over to Mack's bunk.

He was writhing on the mattress, his face rolling from side to side on the pillow. I put my hand on his forehead and felt how hot it was before he twitched away from under my fingers.

"How long has he been like this?" I asked the boy quietly.

"I dunno," he said, sounding scared. "A while I guess."

Mack groaned in pain, his head raising up a little, then thudding back on the pillow. I shone the light on his right hand and saw that his arm, above the bandage, was red and swollen.

"Get in your bed," I said. "I'll take care of it."

"Okay," he said, relieved, and I heard his bare feet pat across the floor boards, then the slight rustle of him climbing between his bedclothes.

I looked at Mack again. His teeth were clenched together tightly and he kept grimacing and making little noises in his throat which, every few moments, became pitiful, drawn-out moans.

"What'sa matter with 'im?" I heard a voice and, shining my light up to the bunk above, I saw Tony raised on one elbow. He blinked and turned his face to the side until I lowered the beam a little.

"Go to sleep, Tony," I said.

"What'sa matter?" he asked. "He sick?"

"Yes," I said. "Now—"

"*Good*," said Tony.

"Tony, that isn't nice," I said firmly.

"I hope he *dies*," said Tony.

"All right, that's enough," I said. "Go to sleep."

I didn't have the time to worry about Tony, so I lowered my flash beam to Mack again. I stood there about a minute, looking down at his slightly thrashing body, the increasing sounds of pain he made. Then I leaned over and put my hand on his shoulder.

"Mack," I said, shaking him a little. "Mack, wake up."

He reared up a little, gasping convulsively, then fell back, eyes wide open and staring at me. I could tell he didn't know who I was. He didn't even seem to know *where* he was.

"Mack, we'd better go down to the dispensary," I said.

He breathed raggedly through an open mouth, staring up at me, his chest rising and falling in quick, shallow movements.

"Mack, you've got a fever. You'd better—"

"What d'ya want?" he asked gutterally.

"You'd better go to the dispensary. Come on, I'll help you."

He knocked my hand off his shoulder as if it were a spider. "Get outta here," he said breathlessly. I noticed how swollen-pupiled his eyes were.

"Mack, get up," I said. "You've got a fever."

He closed his eyes and lay there breathing heavily, mouth open. He rubbed an awkward hand across his brow, breath hissing slowly through gritted teeth.

"Get outta here," he said hoarsely.

"Mack, come on," I told him. "Get up. You've got to—"

"Who's 'at?" he asked, eyes open again, staring up at me.

"It's Matt," I said. "Come on, let's go."

"Matt," he said, as if he were tasting the name, "Matt." He winced and groaned a little, then whimpered with pain. "My hand," he muttered. "Oh, Jesus God, my *hand*."

"Mack, come on. Miss Leiber will fix you up."

He writhed his heavy-muscled shoulders on the mattress and then, with mindlessly irritated fingers, he fumbled and jerked down the zipper of his sleeping bag. I could see that his skin of his chest was flushed and covered with a dew of sweat.

"Hot," he mumbled. "Goddam hot."

"Mack, come on." I put my hand on his arm. "Let's go to—"

His left hand clamped, vise-like, on my wrist and he stared up at me. "Who th'hell *are* ya," he asked.

"Matt Harper," I said.

"Harper," he said, letting go. He made a sound which, I guess, was laughter. "*Harper*," he said. "We'll ge' rid o' you too." Another gasping, mirthless laugh. "Ge' you the hell out same way we got Merv." He grimaced. "Damn queer," he muttered between his teeth, his head stirring fitfully on the pillow again.

I stood looking down at him blankly, listening to him mumble to himself.

"Ge' you too," he said. "You too. All fairies, all ya. We'll get ya." He drew in rasping, phlegmy breath and moaned, "Oh Jesus, Jesus, my *hand!*"

"Mack, come on, let me—"

He knocked my hand off again and I straightened up.

"Took 'is bathrobe," Mack said, chuckling hollowly. "Stubid bastid, never even—"

He shuddered and, suddenly, opened his mouth wide. A long, loud groan filled the cabin.

"Hey, what's that?" asked a boy's thin, frightened voice across the way.

"Nothing," I said. "Go to sleep."

"Who're *you?*"

"The Werewolf of London," I snapped. "Go to sleep, will you?"

I waited a few minutes, then left the cabin and went to the dispensary. Ten minutes of knocking managed to rouse a heavily dormant Miss Leiber who came to the door in her woolly wrapper. I told her Mack was feverish. She asked me why I didn't bring him to the dispensary, and I told her. Clucking disgustedly to herself, she got dressed and went back with me.

When we reached Mack's cabin, we found the lights on and Mack was propped on one elbow, cursing at kids. Miss Leiber shut him up. Then, between the two of us, we got him on his feet and down to the dispensary where she took over.

I walked back to the cabin, thinking of what Mack had mumbled unaware. How nicely, how sickeningly, it all fit together: Merv caught without his robe or towel, the damning evidence Big Ed had sought so long.

I lay awake quite a while, feeling as cold as the moon, thinking of a man named Edward Nolan and how his immediate removal from this world would make so many people so happy.

4.

Madame La Toure ended it.

While we were eating lunch, Jack Stauffer got up at the leader's table and raised his arms for quiet. He was holding a piece of yellow paper in his right hand and he stood there posed like that until talk had ceased. Then he lowered his arms while, seated beside him, Ed Nolan kept on eating.

"We just received a telegram this morning," Jack announced, "in answer to a message we sent to Marie La Toure who, you all know, is the great French high-dive artist."

A buzz of excited talk. "All right, all right, hold it down," said Jack, amiably demanding, his arms raised again. When the boys had quieted down, he read, "*I am delighted to be asked to perform at Camp Pleasant stop Will be happy to do so stop I will be at the camp the morning of August 5th stop Sincerely Madame Marie La Toure.*"

"Yay!" some boys began cheering and it caught on. I sat there thinking about Doc and Ed arguing.

"Now what this means," Jack went on when quiet had more or less ensued, "is that the Madame will be here the day after tomorrow."

He armed down a rising flurry of yays and hand clappings.

"Hold it," he said. "And *that* means we've got a lot of work to do this afternoon and tomorrow to get the camp all cleaned up for the

117

Madame's arrival. We've got to erect an extension to the diving platform and the dock's going to have to be really scrubbed down good, then decorated."

A look of tender recollection came into Jack's eyes.

"I don't know whether any of you have ever seen Madame La Toure perform," he said. "If you have, you know what a treat we're in for. If you haven't well, take it from me, you're going to see one of the *greats* in high-dive artistry. Marie La Toure, although not too well known in this country, is a continental favorite in Europe where she's performed before the crowned heads of England, Norway, Sweden and lots of other nations too numerous to mention."

During rest period, the boys discussed the impending event with enthusiasm; except for Charlie Barnet who seemed more amused than excited. I remembered that this was his sixth year at Camp Pleasant and I asked him if he'd seen Madame La Toure before.

"Huh?"

I repeated.

"Yeah," he said, "I seen her."

"She good?"

He had obvious trouble repressing a smile. "Yeah," he said, "she's pretty good."

Whereupon he was deluged with questions from the boys which he answered carefully, slowly and, I was sure, falsely.

After rest period, we were sent down to the dock to help slick it up and I asked Jack Stauffer about it. He and I were on top of the diving platform, nailing on the beginnings of an extension.

"What's the deal with this Madame La Toure?" I asked.

"Deal?" he asked back, looking surprised.

I nodded, "Yeah. Is there really such a person?"

He looked still more surprised.

"You heard the telegram," he said sincerely. "You don't think I made it up, do you?"

I looked at him carefully. "You pulling my leg?" I asked.

He laughed pleasantly. "You'll see," he said. "She's a magnificent performer."

"Then there really *is* a Madame La Toure?"

"Of course," he said.

※　　※　　※

That evening, Ed Nolan got around to informing me that I was fired. It was after supper and Sid told me that Ed wanted me in the office.

As I went in through the dining hall door, Ed was sitting at his desk, his back to me, thumbing through some papers—the employees' contracts, I noticed as I came closer. I stood beside the desk and he kept thumbing through them. He found mine and, without even glancing up at me, tossed it on the desk.

"You're out," he said. "Sign the bottom line. You'll get ya check in September."

I stood there, motionless, until he looked up.

"I said *sign* it," he told me in that same tone of voice I'd heard when he'd demanded an apology of Merv.

"When am I supposed to leave?" I asked.

"I want ya out o' camp by tomorrow night."

"I'll be out," I said and, leaning over the desk, I signed the dismissal clause at the bottom of the contract, feeling a little sick as I did because I knew that, after the next night, I'd never see Ellen again.

I tossed the pen on the desk and straightened up.

"Now get out o' this office," he said, sounding less imperious than sullen and disgruntled.

"Good night," I said, and left the office. There was no violence left in me. I was just tired of the whole damn business.

※　※　※

It was a Wednesday night and there were movies down in the lodge so I sent my boys there and stayed in the cabin, packing my trunk.

I was folding up some shirts and putting them away when the screen door squeaked open and, looking over my shoulder, I saw Tony standing there.

"Hello," I said.

"Hi, Matt," he said. He came in and walked over to where I was. "What're ya doin'?"

"Nothing. Why aren't you down at the movies?"

"I didn't feel like it."

"Oh." I knew what he really meant was he didn't like to sit among boys who did not welcome him.

"What're ya packin' your trunk for?" he asked.

I decided it wasn't worth the trouble to lie. "I'm leaving," I said.

I didn't see his face but his voice was very surprised. "*Leavin'*?" he said. "Why?"

Again, I saw no reason for lying and I told him I'd been fired by Nolan.

"What for?" he asked, sitting down on the edge of my bunk, looking at me curiously.

I shrugged. "We just don't get along," I said.

"Was it because ya got me outta cleanin' the garbage cans?"

"Oh...I don't think so, Tony. It's more than that."

"Jesus," he said. "That dirty son-of-a—"

"All right, Tony," I cut him off. "Let it go."

He watched in silence a while as I packed.

"How are you getting along?" I asked him.

"What d'ya mean?"

"Are you getting used to being in Mack's cabin?"

He shrugged. "I dunno," he said carelessly.

"You washing your clothes?"

Another shrug. "I s'pose."

"Not having any fights, I hope."

"Not unless I feel like it," said Tony.

I closed my trunk and sat on the top so the lock would catch. I pushed in the catch, then looked up at him.

"I'll miss you, Tony," I said.

He didn't seem to understand. He looked at me blankly. "What d'ya mean?" he asked.

"I mean I like you. We're friends, aren't we?"

"I...guess so."

"Well, I'll be sorry not to see you any more."

"Why?"

"Because we're friends," I said, "and I don't like to leave my friends."

"Oh." He looked at the floor.

"Tony," I said, "will you promise me something?"

He looked up suspiciously. "What?"

"Will you be a good boy the rest of the season? Wash your clothes, don't fight, try to make friends with the other boys?"

"Aaaah, they don't want no friends," he said.

"How do you know?"

He shrugged. "I know," he said.

121

"What about David Lewis?" I asked. "Why don't you make friends with him?"

"*That* pansy?"

"He's a good kid, Tony, don't fool yourself," I said. "He's quiet, that's all."

He stood up. "Well, I gotta go," he said.

I put out my hand. "I may not see you tomorrow to say good-bye, Tony," I said. "So shall we shake hands now?"

He stared at me, not the trace of a smile on his face. Then he came over and shook my hand solemnly. "You got the dirty end o' the stick," he said.

"Don't worry about it, Tony," I said, pushing a friendly fist against his jaw. "Just be good."

"Sure, Matt," he said, and turned away.

I sat on the trunk a long time after he was gone, staring at the screen door. Sure, Matt. Sure, Matt. His last words kept repeating in my mind. Sure, Matt. Sure—and he was damned. His future lay in the hands of a misunderstanding father and in the city streets where he'd play and grow like a weed that breaks through concrete, surviving, not because it's beautiful or good but because it's hardy enough to exist despite every condition which seeks to kill it.

I felt pretty low down that night, thinking of Tony, of Ellen. So low down that I didn't even bother telling the boys that I was leaving. I had them get ready for bed and I went to bed too and lay there awake, feeling lousy.

5.

The next morning, all the boys got dressed in their Sunday clothes for the performance of Madame Marie La Toure, France's contribution to the art of the high dive. I hadn't had much chance to ponder over the existence or non-existence of the woman but it sort of bothered me that morning, despite the growing tension I felt as I approached the moment when I'd have to leave Ellen forever. If the Madame La Toure business were a gag, what in hell was the punch line? For a whole day the boys had knocked themselves out sweeping, mopping, painting, scrubbing, hanging bunting and streamers and a huge painted banner—*WELCOME TO CAMP PLEASANT, MADAME LA TOURE!* Now they were getting dressed in their best clothes, all chattering excitedly—except for Charlie Barnett.

At eleven o'clock, the car arrived bearing Madame La Toure. Everyone was in the great open area in front of the dining hall; all the eager-faced boys, the counselors, the section leaders, the kitchen help, the craft shop personnel and Jack. The only ones who weren't there were the cooks and kitchen helpers and Ed, Ellen, and Doc.

When the convertible turned in off the road, a great cheer billowed up from the boys and the dark-haired woman sitting on top of the back seat in a bathing suit waved at everyone. Without comprehending, I looked at the woman as she got out of the convertible, a robe thrown over her shoulders, and was led by Jack Stauffer into the dining hall to be feted. I walked over to where Bob was.

"What is this?" I asked.

"You don't know?" he asked, a little surprised.

"No. What is it?"

He was going to tell me but then we all had to go into the dining hall for dinner and speeches.

All through the meal, I kept looking at the dark-haired woman eating at the leader's table, wondering what in hell it was all about.

Her speech did nothing to alleviate confusion, her French accent being that of a high-school actress imitating Catherine Deneuve.

"I 'ave zee great 'appiness to be wiz you today," she said, "for zee exhibeeshun. I 'ave always like to perform for zee boys as zey appreciate zo much my diveeng."

I didn't notice the water-front counselors leaving, one by one, during the course of the meal. When dinner had ended, Jack announced that the exhibition would take place and "Yah!" cheered all the boys as I watched the smile of unparalleled ghoulishness on the face of Charlie Barnett. As everyone was filing out of the dining hall and straggling down the hill toward the dock, I caught Bob's arm and took him aside.

"Now what is this?" I asked.

"It's a practical joke," he said, sounding neither dismayed nor amused.

"How does it work?"

"Well, all the kids will be massed on the dock," he said, "shoulder to shoulder. They'll be so packed they won't be able to move. The exit from the dock will be blocked by counselors."

I began to feel strangely worried.

"The woman will climb up to the top of the platform," he said.

"Who is she?" I asked.

"Who knows?" he said. "Some friend of Jack's wife I guess."

"She's not a diver?"

"Not as far as I know," he said. "Even if she is, she's not going to be doing any diving."

"What *does* she do?"

"Well, she'll get to the very top of the extension. Then she'll take off her robe and call down to the boys—*Are you ready?*"

"How do you know all this?" I asked abruptly.

"Merv told me," he said. "He saw it once."

"Oh. So she asks them if they're ready. Then what?"

"Well, that's the key to the whole thing. She keeps asking them—*Are you ready?* and they'll keeping saying—*Yes!* She'll ask them again—Are you *sure* you're ready? and they'll shout again—*Yes!*"

"*Then* what?"

"Then the counselors inside the tower rip open and drop streamers and throw pails of water on all the kids and the counselors on the dock shove them into the lake."

"*What?*"

"That's it," he said, apparently casual.

"But that's *fantastic*," I said. "You mean they're going to push them in the lake with their good clothes on?"

"Sure."

"Oh, come on. Some of those kids can't swim. They'll be scared half to death. And they just *ate*, for Christ's sake. They'll get cramps." I suddenly remembered Doc's words about what had happened the last time.

Bob didn't seem to care. He seemed distracted and oblivious.

"What about your own kids?" I asked. "Doesn't it matter to you if—"

"No, it doesn't," he said, curtly, and turned away.

I looked down the hill at the rapidly accumulating crowd of boys on the dock and a tight, restless feeling started to come over me.

Jack and the young woman went past me.

"Coming?" Jack asked. "If you don't hurry, you won't get a good spot."

Suddenly I thought of David and my body twitched with shock. He'd be scared to death getting drenched first, then shoved into the lake. I started down the hill suddenly, anger rising. Five of the cabin counselors stood at the entrance to the dock, chatting and laughing with Jack and the woman. One of the counselors was Mack.

"Well, if it isn't Harper," he said. "Goin' in t'see the act?"

I didn't say a word but walked past him onto the dock which was becoming jammed with milling boys, all talking excitedly. I bumped into Charlie Barnett who stood near the shore-end of the dock where he'd not only be out of range of the bucket emptiers but be able to jump to shore and run for it when the other counselors started pushing kids into the lake.

"You little rat," I said. "Where's David?"

"Who?" Blandly.

"*David*," I said. "Come on, come on, where *is* he?"

"I dunno. Why?"

"One side, boys, one side!" I heard the cheery voice of Jack Stauffer behind me, and with a spattering of "Yahs!" the boys parted like a sea to let the "Madame" through.

I stepped aside, feeling my heart start to beat heavily. I stood up on my toes, trying to see David. I called his name but was drowned out by the general tumult. I pushed by several boys, searching desperately for David but the ranks had closed tightly behind Jack and I was blocked. I yelled to him but he was too absorbed in conducting the woman to the tower.

"David!" I yelled, on my toes again.

I felt my stomach muscles jolt. He was standing right under the tower.

"Oh, my god," I muttered. I tried to shove through the boys but I couldn't. I called again but David didn't hear me. A sense of panic began to take hold of me coupled with a rising fury at this ultimate in viciousness. I lunged back toward the shore to find someone who could stop it; at least long enough to get David out of there.

Mack and the other counselors were lined up at the end of the dock and Mack held out a blocking palm as I came up to them.

"Where ya goin'?" he asked, trying to sound amiable but failing.

"Look out."

"Don't ya wanna see the divin' show?" he asked.

"Yeah, don't ya wanna see Madame Le Toure?" another counselor asked.

"I said look out, damn it!"

"We got orders not to let anyone off the dock." Mack said.

"So help me God—!" I started, shoving past him.

He grabbed my arm and the other counselor grabbed my other arm.

I jerked the one arm loose but Mack had a stronger grip. I didn't bother talking this time. I drove my left fist as hard as I could into his face and he went back with a cry of pain, bowling over two of the other counselors. I turned and ran up the hill.

I found Sid in the office. He looked up in surprise as I came bursting in. "What *is* it?" he asked quickly.

"Can't you stop this damn thing?" I asked breathlessly.

"I'm afraid not," he said. "It's Ed's idea."

"I thought you didn't know about it," I said.

"Jack just told me this morning," he said.

"Well.... Goddam it, are there any limits in this son-of-a bitch camp?"

"Take it easy, Matt."

"*Easy*! What about Tony? Do you think he's going to take this? And do you know where David Lewis is? Right under the tower! He'll be soaked first and scared to death! Then he'll get shoved into the lake!"

"They won't shove him in if he can't swim."

"What's to keep them from it?"

From the dock, I heard Jack's voice start over the loudspeaker system.

"You can't stop it?" I asked.

"No," he said.

"What about Doc?"

"Maybe, but I doubt it."

"Well, by God, I've *had* it!" I yelled, and turning, I lunged out of the office. Sid called me but I paid no attention. I started running down the path toward Ed Nolan's cabin.

To this day, I don't know what I thought I was going to do to make Nolan stop it. All I knew was that David was down there, not knowing what was coming. And Tony was there and a lot of small kids waiting and I was furious at this last, most outrageous Camp Pleasantry.

The area of woods around the section leaders' tent and Jack Stauffer's cabin was deserted and still as I ran along the path. The only sound was the thumping of my shoes. When I reached the cabin at the end of the path, I jerked open the screen door and ran through the kitchen into the still house.

"Mister Nolan!" I yelled.

No answer. I dashed through the living room onto the porch but that was empty too.

It was when I came back into the living room that I noticed what I hadn't seen at first. The floor and rugs were covered with bright red spots—the kind made by—

Hard cold fingers clutched at my stomach suddenly as I stood there staring at those spots. Then, as if I knew already, I stumbled across the room and shoved open the door.

She was crumpled on the bedroom floor in a new white dress and white shoes and white gloves. Only none of them were white because they were covered with blood. With a sick gasp, I started forward, staring at her still face. Then, as I bent over her, she groaned a little and I smelled the heavy fumes of whiskey on her breath.

That was when I saw him from the corners of my eyes and my head jerked up, a sudden wave of horror breaking over me.

Ed Nolan was lying motionless on the blood-soaked bed, the handle of a hunting knife protruding from his throat.

1.

When Sid and I came out of the Emmetsville police station that afternoon, he suggested we have a cup of coffee before driving back to camp.

We went to the same drugstore Mack, Bob and I had been in that first night. I even sat on the same counter stool and the same girl brought me coffee in the same kind of cup. There the similarities ended. The first time I hadn't even met Ellen; this time I loved her and she was in jail under suspicion of murdering her husband. Two cups of coffee with a lifetime of emotions between them.

"Doc staying at the station?" I asked as I drizzled sugar into my cup.

Sid nodded. "We'll go back without him," he said. "He has his own car."

Silent drinking awhile. The clink of coffee cups, the sounds of a drugstore on a sleepy summer afternoon: the occasional slap of the screen door, the mumbling and laughter of two small boys in the front of the store looking at comic books, the rattle of dishes in the back kitchen, the monotonous whir of the wall fan as it turned from side to side. Life going on for everyone except a frightened girl a few blocks away who didn't know if she had killed her husband.

"I just can't see her doing it," I said. "She's so—" I broke off and stared into the cup.

"Drink can change a person," Sid said. "Change them a lot. They'll do things that, sober, they wouldn't even dream of doing; and, if they drink enough, they'll do things they won't even remember doing."

"I just can't see that," I said. "To kill somebody—like *that*—then not even remember it?"

He drew in a slow breath.

"I was drunk once," he said, "I mean really drunk. In the army; years ago. I got drunk on Saturday afternoon and the next thing I knew it was Sunday night. I was in a hotel bed with two women and there was an inch-long gash on my head. And I didn't remember a thing about it."

I put down my cup. "If the case is as clear as all that, why are the police asking questions?"

He shrugged. "It's the way they do it, I guess," he said.

"No," I said. "No, it's more than that. They kept asking me questions about Ed's relationships to everybody in the camp. Why should they if they knew it was Ellen?"

"They're probably just making sure, Matt," he said, looking at me. "I wouldn't lay too much emphasis on it. I don't want to think she did it any more than you do but—well, the facts speak for themselves."

"What facts?"

"She was right there beside him, Matt," he said, "covered with blood."

"She could be right there covered with blood if she found him too," I said.

"I don't know, Matt," he said.

"And what about the knife?" I kept on. "It belongs to that kid in Bob's cabin, doesn't it?"

"What does that prove?"

"If she killed Ed, why didn't she use one of the kitchen knives?"

"I don't know, Matt," Sid said, obviously not wanting to discuss it. "Maybe she found it. The kid lost the knife a week before—it happened."

"No, it doesn't make sense," I said, getting angry with Sid because I had to let it out on someone.

"Maybe you don't want to see the sense of it," he said.

"What does that man?" I asked.

"I wouldn't even mention it, if this thing hadn't happened," he said. "I'm not a guy to meddle in other people's business, but—" he cleared his throat—"I saw you come out of the Nolan cabin one afternoon a few weeks ago." He glanced at me. "You looked pretty shaky, Matt."

"What are you trying to say?" I asked.

"The police are looking for reasons Ed was killed," he answered. "Are you sure you don't know the reason?"

"No," I said, "I don't."

"She was trying to leave Ed that afternoon," he said. "At least she was planning to leave; there was a packed suitcase locked in the bedroom closet."

"I didn't know that," I said.

He nodded. "Doc told me," he said. "The way I see it, Ed caught her trying to leave and locked up her suitcase. She went in the bathroom with a bottle and got drunk, worked herself into a pitch, found Ed sleeping on the bed and—"

"What about all the blood in the living room?" I asked.

"He was a big guy," Sid answered. "He probably staggered around."

"Well, what—"

"The point of all this is," he interrupted, "something made Ellen decide to leave Ed."

"And you think I'm that something?"

"Are you, Matt?"

"There's never been anything intimate between us if that's what you think," I said. "She's not that kind. Neither am I."

"All right," he said. "I'm sorry I brought it up."

"We were—drawn to each other," I said, not able to stop myself. "We had similar interests. Books, music—"

I stopped and looked at Sid.

"Oh, why lie about it?" I said. "I'm in love with her. And I think she loves me. But there was never any decision made as far as Ed was concerned. I should have had the courage to make a positive move but I didn't. I guess maybe I was never sure until now."

I pushed away the coffee cup and stared at my hands on the counter.

"You see," I said, "I was engaged to this girl. She died in an auto accident about a year ago. I thought maybe I was—just trying to forget about *her*. I know now that's not true. I know I didn't even love this other girl. Not the same way. I was mixed up with—selfishness, I guess I'll have to call it. I was going to get a fancy job in her father's plant. When she died it was as if—God, how lousy it sounds—as if my security were dying too. I never knew that till I fell in love with Ellen. Because there's nothing like that involved with her. No...package deal like the other one." I shook my head. "Far from it," I said.

I turned to him.

"This has nothing to do with the—murder," I told him. "I just want you to know it isn't what you may think it is—something cheap. I want to marry her, Sid. I *will* marry her."

Sid didn't say anything for a while. We sat quietly and, every few

134

seconds, the breeze from the fan would ruffle my hair and then the breeze would be gone, leaving me in warm, stale air.

"Let's go," Sid said finally.

We left and drove back to camp in the truck. We didn't speak anymore except when Sid told me, "Oh, about your being fired. Doc told me that, as long as the camp keeps running—which may not be long—you'll stay with your cabin."

"All right," I said.

2.

It was just before supper. I was laying on the bunk, staring up at Chester Wickerly's slowly swinging legs. The cabin was quiet. All the other boys were down in front of the mess hall waiting for the buzzer to sound.

The screen door rasped open and, looking over, I saw Tony come in carrying an armful of clothes and his *Louisville Slugger* which he dumped on his old bunk.

"Hi," he said, sounding rather belligerent.

I stared at him. "What—?" I started.

"I'm back," he said.

"Back?"

"Yeah."

"How come?"

He shrugged carelessly. "Just wanna," he said.

"But, no one has said anything about—"

"He can't stop me."

"Who?"

"The fat guy."

I was on my elbow now, looking at Tony carefully, trying to figure a way out of this. "Did anyone tell you to come back?" I asked.

"I'm comin' back," was all he said.

"But have you asked anyone? Doc? Sid?"

"They ain't the leader!" he said hotly, his lips pressed together adamantly. "I'm comin' back."

The dinner buzzer. We looked at each other, Tony trying to stare me down.

Chester Wickerly jumped down on the floor. "Chow," he said. Tony paid no attention nor did I. "Goin' t'chow?" asked Chester.

"Go on," I said. "I'll be right there."

Chester shrugged. "Okay." He started for the door, telling Tony en route, "This ain't your cabin, Rocca." Tony's resort was unprintable. So was Chester's deft return as he departed for chow.

I got up. "Tony, you can't take things into your own hands like this," I told him.

"I'm comin' back, damn it!" he yelled, the skin tightening suddenly over his gaunt face. A great tear fell across his cheek. He brushed it off furiously, choking on his breath.

"All right, Tony, all right," I said, putting my arm around his thin shoulders. "I'll talk to Sid about it. Maybe we can get you back."

"I'm *comin'* back," he muttered.

"That's enough. I'll do what I can but I'm still the head of this cabin. Understand?"

Silence; a spasmodic sniff.

"Do you?"

"O-*kay*," he acceded, then added a trembling, "Chris*sake*."

"Come on," I said. "Let's go eat." I held him close to me as we left the cabin.

3.

That night there was a special meeting of all the counselors, kitchen workers and Miss Leiber. Bob and I went to the mess hall together, finding chairs lined up, Cokes in front of each one. Doc was sitting at a table at the head of the room going through some papers. I hadn't seen him in days and the change in him was shocking. I'd never really thought of Doc in terms of age but I couldn't help it that night.

Before the meeting started, I went over to Sid and told him about Tony.

"You think Doc will mind if he transfers back to my cabin?" I asked. "There doesn't seem much reason for him not to now."

Sid nodded restlessly. "All right," he said. "Just tell Riley about it."

I rejoined Bob.

"Wonder what this is all about," he said.

"I don't know," I said, taking a sip of the icy Coke. I thought about Ellen waiting in that jail cell. It was horrible to sit there thinking about it, unable to help her at all.

Doc stood up when everybody was there and seated, his voice slow and tired.

"First of all," he said. "As temporary head of the camp, I wanted to thank all of you for keeping the camp schedule going as if nothing had happened. Believe me, it's appreciated."

He took a slow breath, looking down at the papers on the table. Then he looked up again.

"The reason we're here is this: I don't know if the camp is going to finish out the season or not. We've been flooded with calls from the boys' parents. Some of them have already made cancellations. That's what these are," he said, holding up the papers. "Sid will hand them out to you after I'm finished. I'm afraid there'll be more. If there are too many the camp will have to close.

"I got a call from the Board this evening. They're very doubtful about continuing. I managed to talk them into delaying their decision but—well, it all depends on the parents."

Again he stared down at the papers and we sat waiting. He seemed to have been broken by Ed's death, his vitality drained. While we sat waiting for him to go on, I heard Mack clear his throat and heard someone else's feet shuffle momentarily. Doc looked up.

"To those of you who chipped in and bought flowers and candy for Mrs. Nolan," he said, "I want to extend my personal thanks. I don't think I have to tell you what it meant to her."

That had been Sid's idea. The day after Ed's death, he'd come around during rest period, getting money from the counselors in order to send something to Ellen. Apparently, he hadn't told Doc it was his idea.

"As far as the tragedy is concerned," Doc went on with obvious difficulty, "we've engaged a lawyer to defend Mrs. Nolan and there is every hope that...." He broke off and tried to straighten his shoulders without much success. "Well," he said, "Let's not lose hope for her."

He looked around at us all.

"I think that's about all," he said. "As far as what I have to say anyway. All we can do is wait and go on as if nothing has happened. For your efforts in that direction, my thanks to all of you."

After Jack had brought up a few inane points about the water-front schedule, Sid had handed out the cancellations to the counselors involved (one to Bob, one to me—David Lewis). Then after Barney Wright had gotten up and, simply and beautifully, pronounced his faith in Ellen, the meeting broke up.

Bob and I were going out when I felt someone touch my arm and, turning, saw Miss Leiber.

"Yes?" I asked.

"I'd like to speak to you," she said. She glanced at Bob. "Privately."

"All right."

I said goodnight to Bob and Miss Leiber and I walked along the dark path toward the dispensary.

"What is it?" I asked her, but she wouldn't tell me until we'd reached the dispensary and she'd closed the door firmly behind her. Then she turned to me and said, "It's about your friend."

"My—"

"I don't believe I remember his name. The young fellow you were just with."

"Bob Dalrymple," I said.

She nodded. "Yes," she said, "Dalrymple."

"What about him?" I asked.

"The day of the—" She broke off nervously. "The day Mister Nolan died," she amended, "I saw your friend Dalrymple go by here." Her lips pressed together for a moment. "He was heading for the Nolan cabin."

I stared at her a second or two without comprehending. Then it hit me. "*What time?*" I asked.

"Just before *you* came by."

"Oh." I looked at her dazedly.

"I haven't told anyone," Miss Leiber said. "I didn't want to involve him when I wasn't sure. But I have to tell someone; it's not fair to Mrs. Nolan for me to remain silent if what I know might help her."

She drew in a quick breath. "The reason I'm telling you instead of Phillip," she said (it was odd to hear Doc called that), "is that you're the young man's best friend and I think you should determine if there's any significance to what I saw. If there isn't, we can forget it and your friend won't be hurt in any way."

She swallowed with effort.

"But if there *is*," she said. For once, Miss Leiber didn't sound in absolute command of herself.

I walked back along the path, feeling the cold night air through my zelan jacket. *Best friend*. The phrase depressed me. How could I feel this sort of shackled elation at the possibility that a best friend had committed murder?

When I reached Bob's cabin, he wasn't there. I walked up to Paradise but he wasn't there either. I decided he must have gone to *The Crossroads Tavern* for a hamburger. I got ready for bed and lay there awake until I heard footsteps outside. Then I got up and went out.

"Bob?" I called softly.

He turned and, seeing me, waited until I'd come down the porch steps and over to where he was standing.

"What's up?" he asked.

I didn't want to drag it out for a second. "Were you in Ed's cabin the day he died?" I asked.

His face seemed to go slack in the cold moonlight. "What?" he asked.

"You heard me."

I heard him swallow dryly, then make a weak scoffing sound. "Who told you that?" he asked.

"Bob, were you?"

"No," he said.

"Listen," I said, "I'm not trying to trap you. Miss Leiber said she saw you going toward Ed's cabin that day."

"You haven't told anyone about it, have you?" he asked.

"Now *listen*," I said sharply, then realized that someone in the cabins might hear. I took him by the arm and we moved down the hill a little.

"Look, Bob," I said, "I want to know. Were you there?"

His breath was shaky. "Jesus, you don't think *I* did it, do you?" he asked in a horrified whisper. "I didn't even go *in* the cabin."

"You didn't see him then?" I asked.

"I didn't see anybody," he said.

"Then why so secretive?" I asked. "If you had nothing to hide why the hell didn't you tell somebody?"

He was silent a moment, then he said, "I—I saw you coming down to the cabin that day and I didn't want you to know that—"

"That *what*?" My voice was hard; I couldn't help it.

"That I was going down there to quit," he said. "At the last minute, I couldn't do it. I started back for the dock. Then I saw you coming and I just didn't want you to know about it."

"So you hid," I said.

He nodded.

"That's great," I said, "*Great*."

He looked at me curiously. "What are you so upset about?" he asked.

I felt a weight pulling me down as I knew that, in spite of the fact that Bob was my friend, I'd been hoping that he *was* responsible for Ed's death.

"Matt?" he said as I turned away.

I stopped without looking back. "What?"

"You're...not going to tell the—"

"What for?" I said.

"What about Miss Leiber?"

"Tell her what you told me," I said.

"Matt, I can't," he said, worried. "Can't you?"

I looked over my shoulder at him. "All right," I said, "I'll tell her."

4.

There was another meeting three days later. Three days of boys being taken home, of camp life staggering toward a complete halt. Three days closer to Ellen's trial.

I think we all knew what this meeting was about. We filed into the Dining Hall and took our seats. There were no Cokes this time, just grim silence. We all waited, looking at the table where Doc sat.

At last he stood. He looked even worse than he had at the first meeting.

"I guess you all know what we're here for," he said slowly. He gestured toward the papers on the table. We knew what they were without him saying. "The director of the board called this evening. We're going to have to close the camp."

Dead silence for a long moment. I glanced aside at the grim faces of the counselors near me.

"The buses will arrive here Saturday morning about eleven," Doc went on. "Until then we'll have to start preparing for the shutdown. Your section leaders will give you the details."

Another silence. Doc stood there looking lost.

"I'm sorry, boys," he said, and sat down.

When the meeting had ended, Bob asked me if I wanted to go to the *Crossroads* but I said no. He left without another word and I went over to Doc.

"How is she?" I asked him.

He exhaled slowly. "As well as possible, son," he said.

"What—what does her lawyer think?" I asked, "About her chances, I mean."

Doc shook his head. "I don't know, son," he said. "He's doing all he can."

"I see." I turned away.

I was going up the cabin steps when I heard my name called softly. Turning my head, I saw a shadowy figure rise from the steps of the next cabin and move toward me. When I got close enough, I saw it was Sid.

"I forgot to tell you," he said, "those of us staying for the trial will live here in camp, probably in the section leaders' tent."

"Oh. All right."

He looked at me a moment, then said, "You want to talk about it?"

"Talk?"

"Maybe it'll help," he said.

I didn't understand what he meant but when he said, "Come on," I followed him over to the big stump in front of my cabin and sat down beside him.

"I think you should prepare yourself," he told me, "since you say you feel as you do. Ellen's the only suspect. She had every reason to do it. No matter what you feel toward her you have to recognize the facts."

"How do you go about preparing yourself for something like that?" I asked him.

"I...know it isn't much consolation, but her lawyer is pretty certain there won't be any capital punishment," Sid told me. "I'm sure he'll plead temporary insanity, maybe even self-defense. After all, Matt, the thing isn't one-sided. The law recognizes mental state in a case like this; and if anyone can be defended on those grounds, it's Ellen Nolan."

"You're convinced she did it then," I said.

He didn't answer soon enough.

"Never mind," I said.

"Matt, you may as well face it. I don't like to think about it any more than you do. But there's no one else who could have done it. You know that." He made a scoffing sound. "I came here to try and cheer you up and—" He broke off and slapped his palm a couple of times with the flashlight. "I guess I haven't helped very much," he said.

"I appreciate it," I said. "I can't help it if I—oh, I don't know." I stood up abruptly and slid my hands into my pockets.

"Going to bed?" he asked me.

"I suppose," I said. "I won't sleep though."

"Try to get some rest," he said. "You'll need it. We have a rough few days ahead getting ready to clear out. Then there'll be the trial."

I nodded. "Goodnight, Sid."

"Goodnight, kid," he said. "Try to rest."

"All right."

I moved up the steps as he rose and walked away toward the bridge. As I entered the cabin, I heard a rustling sound to my left and, looking over, I saw the dark outline of Tony sliding under his covers. I went over to his bunk.

"You been listening?" I asked.

He must have heard the tense sound in my voice. "Uh-uh," he said.

I blew out a long stream of jaded breath. "Tony, the camp is closing this Saturday. Will you do me a favor and tell the truth until then?"

"*Closing?*" It was the first time I'd ever heard him sound shocked.

"Yes."

"*Why?*"

"You know why."

He lay there silently looking up at me. Then I heard him swallowing. "I was...listenin'," he said.

"Thank you. Why were you?"

"I...heard ya talkin' about the leader's wife."

"That's no answer, Tony."

"She goin' t'stir?" he asked.

I stared down at him a moment. "Oh, go to sleep," I said.

"*Is* she?"

"What?"

"Goin' t'stir?"

I took in a shaking breath. "Tony, I don't *know*. Now will you shut up and get to sleep?" Even I could hear the tremor in my voice.

He didn't say any more. I lay down on my bed fully clothed and slept about an hour later. I dreamed that Ellen and I had escaped together and were being chased through the woods. Snarling dogs kept catching up to us, and I kept kicking them aside. Ellen held on to me, crying and helpless, and we ran and ran but we never got away. Then Ellen tripped and fell into a deep hole and I grabbed for her but she fell away and I saw her face receding from me.

I woke up with a jolt and sat there, staring dumbly, hearing the birds singing in the gloom of early morning.

I had to see her.

5.

The visiting room in the Emmetsville jail was dingy. It was bare, the floor boards naked and scratched. The walls were rough plaster and there was one high window, wire-covered, opening on a shadow-dim alley. In the center of the room was a heavy oak table with one chair on each side of it and a partition in the middle.

Ellen was on the other side of the table when I was ushered into the room. Behind Ellen, standing with her back to the door which led to the cells, stood a bulky, gray-haired matron, arms crossed, face expressionless.

I felt a sinking in my stomach when I saw the matron. I had known all the time that Ellen and I wouldn't be alone together, yet the sight of that cheerless-looking woman made me more tense than I already was.

Behind me, the door to the station room closed as I walked to the table, hoping that the smile I gave Ellen didn't look as strained as it felt to me. Our hands met over the partition, hers cool and strengthless.

"No more contact, please," the matron said in a bored voice and our hands fell away hastily. Ellen's smile faded, then was restored with a compulsive effort.

"How are you, Ellen?" I asked.

"I'm okay, Matt," she said, "thank you."

We stood there awkwardly a moment, looking at each other, trying to smile and not much succeeding.

Then she said, "Well...." and we both sat down together. I noticed how pale she looked, how dark the circles were around her eyes. She clasped white hands on the table top. The gray smock she wore was clean and pressed but it looked wrong and ugly on her slender body. I sat staring at her. I couldn't think of a thing to say.

"How are things in camp?" Ellen asked.

"We're—closing up," I said, hesitantly. "Too many cancellations. The—parents all taking their kids home."

"I know," she said, looking down at her hands, "I guess you can't blame them, really."

"I suppose not," I said. "But—" I stopped and drew in a fast breath. "Well, never mind about that," I said. "Tell me how you've been."

She smiled sadly. "What can I say? They've treated me very fairly here. And Doc has been—so wonderful. I wish someone would make him rest."

Silence. Our eyes held and, for a moment, it didn't seem to matter that someone strange was in the room with us. My hand twitched empathetically as I cut off the impulse to reach out for her.

"I'm sorry I didn't come before," I said. "I wanted to."

"I know you've been busy," she said. I could hardly hear her voice.

Our eyes held again.

"It's been awful, Ellen," I said. "Going on with the kids. Pretending everything was the same. Eating with them, talking with them, answering their questions."

"I know, Matt," she said.

"*Have* you been all right?" I asked.

"It's not too bad," she said. "I've more or less resigned myself to it. I'm trying to believe it's all for the—"

"I don't want you to believe that," I said.

Her eyes shut and I saw her white throat move painfully.

"Thank you, Matt," she said.

"I'm going to be with you all through it," I told her.

She looked up, an expression of conflict on her face. "Matt, I know you mean well but—"

"Ellen, *don't*," I cut her off. "I'm staying with you; no matter what happens."

The skin drew taut across her pale cheeks and, for a second, there was pain-stricken life in her eyes.

"Matt, I don't *want* you to," she said. "You don't know about me. What if I did it? What if I *did* it, Matt?"

"I love you, Ellen," I said. She started to say something but I stopped her. "Let's not argue about that any more," I said. "It's established."

There was a glistening in her eyes. "Thank you, Matt. Thank you," she barely whispered. "I...if I could tell you what that means to me—I would. But—" She swallowed and bit her lower lip. "Matt." It was all she could say. "*Matt*." And I knew that, no matter what had been unsaid, the visit had served its purpose. When we were separated fifteen minutes later, there was a look of almost peace on her face.

But then the door shut her away from me and I was alone again, shapeless terror returning again like a fever which has broken for a moment, only to return again, worse than ever.

1.

On the way back to camp, I stopped off at *The Crossroads Tavern* for a hamburger and a cup of coffee. It wasn't dark enough yet for the table lights or the lights over the fireplace and the room was dim, the small dance floor laced with shadows.

I was drinking my coffee when I heard the screen door open and two sets of footsteps moving across the barroom into the shadowy room where I was. I looked up. At first, I didn't recognize them. Then it hit me with a rush. The shorter of the two was Jackie.

The other was Merv Loomis.

The instant I pushed to my feet, they stopped and looked at me. As we stood staring at each other, I saw Merv say something and then the two of them turned hastily and left the room. I pushed out of the booth and started across the floor. I heard the screen door close loudly and I started running. Outside, I could hear their shoes moving rapidly down the gravel path.

"Hey, what about ya bill?" the man at the bar called as I started for the door.

I should have told him I'd be right back but I wasn't thinking. I fumbled in my pocket, and realized that I didn't have enough change. Jerking out my wallet, I pulled a dollar bill from it and slapped it on the bar.

"What about ya *change?*" the man called after me but I was already outside.

They were gone. I jumped down the three steps and sprinted down the path for the road. When I reached it, they weren't in sight.

I stood there panting, looking up and down the road with confused eyes, my heart jolting heavily. They couldn't have disappeared so quickly. I raced for the cross-roads, then reversed direction and started the other way toward the Bramblebush Restaurant and the Shady Haven Motel. As I ran along the edge of the road, looking to each side, a scene kept moving through my mind. A scene I hadn't thought of for some time, but a scene that suddenly seemed to promise the answer I'd been looking for so desperately. Merv stumbling away from Camp Pleasant, nose bleeding, a hysterical look on his face. Merv's voice, gasping. I could hear the words as if he were speaking them again in my mind.

He'll pay.

I ran a few yards past the motel before it struck me. Then I dashed back and went into the office. It was empty. I slapped down the button on the desk bell and it broke the stillness. In the back room, I heard someone groan as if getting up from a chair. There was a slap of loose slippers on the floor boards. An old man came out, adjusting spectacles over his pale blue eyes. He shuffled to the counter.

"Sign outside says no vacancies, young man," he said. "Guess ya didn't see it."

"Have you a couple of men living here?" I said.

"Couple o' men?" The old man looked blank.

"One's named Jack something or other," I said. "The other one's named Loomis, Merv Loomis."

"Loomis," said the old man, pondering, "Loomis."

"May I see your book?"

His lips pursed. "No Loomis here."

"Are you sure?"

"Young man, I been in the motel business since before you was born. Think I ought t'know if—"

"May I see your book?" I said.

"Already told ya," he said. "Got no Loomis here. You try the Dan Boone Motel coupla miles west. Manager's John Saylor, friend o' mine. He'll—"

"Is there anyone here named Jack then?" I insisted.

"What's the first name?"

I gritted my teeth. "*Jack* is the first name," I said impatiently.

Blowing out an undisguised breath of disgust, the old man reached down under the counter and came up grunting with a heavy log book.

"No Loomis here," he said. "Told ya that already."

I grabbed for the book but he pulled it away testily.

"Now, you look here, young man," he started.

"Will you please look!" I begged. "This is important!"

He pressed irritated lips together, then flipped open the cover and, mumbling, looked for the current week. He adjusted his spectacles, tugged at his sleeves. I died while he perused the pages carefully, shaking his head.

"No Loomis," he finally said.

"Is there a Jack something then?" I asked.

Lips pursed again.

"Well," he said slowly, "there's a...Jack Wakefield in Cabin Eight."

"Is he alone?" I asked quickly.

"No," he said. "No. Has a friend stayin' with him."

"What's his name?"

"Name," he mumbled. He looked carefully at the page. "Name's...Larkin. Martin Larkin."

"Cabin Eight," I said, turning for the door.

"Don't think they're *in*," the old man called after me.

"They're in," I said. The screen door slapped shut behind me and my shoes crunched over the gravel-strewn court. I stopped by the alley-way between cabins Seven and Eight and a breath of partial relief shuddered through me. I stood there a moment looking at Jackie's tan coupe.

Then I heard a voice inside the cabin—Jackie's. "Well, I just don't see the point," he said.

Silence.

"Oh, come on now," Jackie said. "What are you worrying about? He can't—"

"Be *quiet*," I heard Merv's voice break in, urgently.

"Why?"

"I thought I heard something."

He had. I was on the porch by then, knocking on the door. There was a gasp inside. I stood there in silence, looking at the window curtain fluttering in the breeze.

"Who's there?" I heard Jackie ask.

"Open the door," I said.

Silence, then tentative footsteps. I heard Merv suddenly whisper, "No, don't!" and Jackie's answering scoff, "Oh, Merv."

The door opened. "Well, hello there," Jackie greeted me. "Would you like to—"

I pushed past him.

"Well, *do* come in," he said.

Merv was standing by the bed, dressed in denims and a short-sleeve shirt. The humor was gone from his eyes; there was only dull resentment left.

"Hello, Merv," I said.

"What do you want?" he asked.

"Why did you run away?" I asked.

"That's my affair," he said. "I don't see where you have the right to follow me around."

"I thought we were friends, Merv," I said. "Why should you run away from me?"

"What is it you want?" he asked. Behind me, I heard Jackie close the door with a sigh of resignation.

"I want to know why you're still here," I said.

"I hardly think that's any of your—"

"Come off it, Merv," I said. "You're in trouble."

"Mister Harper, why don't you—?" Jackie started, but I cut him off.

"I asked you why you ran off, Merv," I said. "You didn't answer me."

"I had no desire to see you," he said, trying to sound assured, although I knew he wasn't. The constant movement of his throat showed that.

"Why, Merv?" I asked.

"Listen, Harper, I don't have to explain my movements to you!" he flared.

"Either you explain them to me or you'll explain them to the sheriff!"

His lean face went blank. "What?"

"The sheriff?" Jackie said. "What in the name of God are—"

153

"You were going away, Merv," I said. "You were fired and you said you were going away. But you're still here—and Ed Nolan is dead."

His face went slack. "You—you think that—"

"Why are you here?" I asked. "You said you were going away."

"That's *my* business."

"Not any more it isn't," I answered.

"Oh, this is *impossible!*" Jackie said.

"Why are you still here?" I persisted.

"Get out of this cabin," Merv told me. "I will not be—"

"All right, *don't* tell me," I said. "We'll let the sheriff get it out of you."

He looked stunned again.

"I want facts," I said. "You're in a bad position. Either you tell me or you tell the sheriff. That's *it.*"

Merv swallowed. He glanced at Jackie who was breathing fitfully, left hand pressing against his chest.

"Do you think I killed Ed Nolan?" Merv asked.

"Can you give me one good reason why I shouldn't think it?" I said.

"Good God, what do you take me for?" he said loudly. "Do you think I could do a thing like that?"

"You hated him," I said.

"I *still* hate him," he said. "But I had nothing to do with—"

"I'm not going to argue with you, Merv," I said. "Can you prove you were somewhere else when it happened?"

Merv still looked dazed. "I...I don't know," he said. "It happened so long ago."

"Not so long," I said.

"Well...." Merv looked helplessly toward Jackie. "I—I don't know where we were but—"

"Undoubtedly *here*," Jackie said pettishly. "We rarely rise before noon."

"Why did you come back?" I asked, my confidence slipping.

"I told you," Merv said, "that's my business."

All the tension seemed to explode in me.

"Well, the hell with you!" I found myself yelling at him. "I'm not going to waste my time on you any more! You can be as coy as you like with the sheriff!"

I jerked open the door but Merv was across the room suddenly, his hand tight on my arm. He shoved the door closed.

"*No*," he said. "I don't want to be—involved."

A slow rise of elation in me again.

"Why? If you're innocent, why should you care?"

"I don't want you to tell the sheriff," he said slowly, and there was something more than pleading in his voice.

"Give me one reason why I shouldn't," I said.

He swallowed. "I was not involved in Ed Nolan's death," he said.

My stomach muscles jerked in tautly. "That's for the sheriff to decide," I said, turning the door knob.

His swing came as a total surprise. If he'd been the physical type like Mack, it might have worked. As it was, his fist only grazed my chin and made me fall, off balance, against the door. I grabbed his flailing right arm and spun him around, locking it behind his back. Our shoes scraped wildly on the floor boards and Merv gasped with pain.

"Stop that!" Jackie cried shrilly.

"I want an answer, Merv," I said.

"You *filthy*—" His voice broke off into a sobbing grunt of pain as I jerked up his arm.

"The *story*!" I snarled, feeling as if I could kill him where he stood.

"You filthy brute!" Jackie cried, shivering impotently.

"I didn't kill Ed Nolan!" Merv gasped.

"Then why were you afraid of me calling the sheriff?"

"I can't—" Another twist of his arm. "Will you *stop* it!" he cried hysterically.

"God dam you, I'll snap your arm right off if you don't answer me!" I said, beyond sympathy, beyond reason. It was as if he were pushing Ellen toward her death and didn't care.

"All *right*!" he said with a sharp break in his voice.

I let go abruptly and he stumbled toward the bed, sobbing.

"You filthy—" Jackie started to say, but I cut him off with a, "Shut up, damn it!"

"Uh!"

Merv clumped down on the bed, his thin chest jerking with breaths. I should have felt sorry for him but I couldn't.

"You're like all of them," he said in a trembling voice. "Like every one of them—blind, thoughtless. Without the sensitivity you were born with, without—"

"All right, cut the babbling," I interrupted. "I want an answer to my question."

His head lifted; his eyes burned into me.

"Why did I come back?" he asked, teeth gritted.

I tensed, anticipating.

"Because I was sick of fighting it," he said. "Because I—" he forced it out—"wasn't going to go home to my mother like a—defeated boy."

I stared at him blankly.

"I *was* halfway home," he went on brokenly. "Then—I knew I couldn't face her. So I sent her a—a wire and said I'd left the camp and was going on a trip to the coast." He swallowed. "And I came back here."

"*Why?*" I was too far gone; I really didn't know.

His lips shook. "You won't leave me anything, will you?" he said, his voice as bitter as any voice I've heard in my life.

"I—"

"I came back to Jackie!" He flung the words at me in a spasm of rage and shame.

I started to say something but words didn't come.

"Are you *happy* now?" Merv asked me. "Happy you blundered in and forced it out of me? Happy to find out that I'm—" He didn't finish the sentence. He looked at me accusingly. "Well, what are you waiting for?" he lashed out. "Don't you know enough? Do I have to give you details? Do I have to draw you an outline of—*oh God, I hate what life is*! I hate it!"

I felt something draining from me. It was hope.

"I don't want the police to get my name because if they got my name it would appear in the papers and my mother would see it," Merv went on mechanically. "Is that clear enough? I don't want my mother to know that—" The masochistic impulse departed suddenly. "Oh damn your filthy interference!" he sobbed at me.

My heartbeat was different now, a slow, metronomic beat in my chest. Merv raised his defeated eyes.

"*Well?*" he asked. "Are you going to call the sheriff? Are you still going to...."

I drew in a shaky breath. "I don't know," I said. I wanted to believe he'd killed Ed Nolan and yet I couldn't. I had no evidence to the contrary. I could still call the sheriff. There was still the motive, the possibility. But the assurance was gone.

"Go ahead," said Merv, cutting at his own foundations again. "What's the difference now? I don't care. I just don't care."

"Sweetie, don't say that," Jackie begged suddenly, hurrying to the bed and sitting down beside him. He picked up Merv's lifeless hand and stroked it. I turned and walked slowly across the room.

"What are you going to do?" Jackie asked. "If you have a drop of decency in you, you'll let this thing go. I'll testify he was with me the day it happened. We *were* together. Here."

I said nothing.

"Well?" Jackie asked. I turned at the door and looked over at them. They were watching me like a husband and wife whose home life has been threatened.

"I don't know," I said.

Merv's head fell forward. "It's over," he muttered.

"Sweetie!"

As I trudged across the court, I could hear the voice of Jackie in Cabin Eight. It soothed, it comforted.

✖   ✖   ✖

When I reached the camp I found Sid in the office. I handed him the truck keys and told him what had happened.

"Have you called the sheriff?" he asked me when I finished.

"I don't know what to do," I said.

"If there's the slightest possibility," he said, "we have to follow it up. You know that."

I nodded.

"I think we'd better," he said quietly.

"Would you—?"

"I'll take care of it," he said. "Cabin Eight, Shady Haven Motel?"

"Yes." I stood watching him as he wrote it down on a pad.

"Where are the kids?" I asked.

"In the Lodge," he said, "watching the movies. Oh, incidentally, I'm afraid your cabin's fallen a little behind in getting ready for the close-up. You'll have to push them tomorrow."

"I will," I said.

"Well...get a good night's sleep," he said.

"Okay. Goodnight, Sid."

"Goodnight, kid."

2.

It was to be the last complete day of camp life but Willie Pratt was not inspired. His reveille was as grotesquely ragged as ever. I tossed back the blankets with a hollow sigh and let my legs down over the side of the bunk.

"What's this?" I muttered.

Tony was sitting on the edge of the bunk, dressed, leaning on his *Louisville Slugger*, his legs kicking a little.

"How long have you been up?" I asked.

He shrugged, that look of bitterness on his features. I figured it was best to leave him alone so I got up and went around patting each groaning sleeper.

"Come on," I told them, "Let's go. There's a lot of work to do."

"That's all we *did* yesterday was work!" said Charlie Barnett. I paid no attention. I got dressed and walked up to Paradise to get cleaned up.

At breakfast Tony sat jabbing a spoon into his cereal, hardly eating a mouthful.

"You'd better eat something, Tony," I said. "We have a lot of work to do today."

"Don't wanna."

"You'll get hungry."

"The hell with it," he muttered.

My boys were behind on the cabin so, outside of a little work in the dining hall that afternoon, the cabin itself had top priority.

After breakfast came a G.I. party. Two buckets of soapy water and stiff-bristled brushes scrubbed at the floor boards started it going. While this was going on, the Moody boys were outside with brooms, poking at the eaves, knocking down dead leaves, dust and spider webs.

I should have known better than to have Tony and Marty Gingold working together but I wasn't thinking very accurately those days and I had them out policing the area around the cabin.

Jim Moody was the first to announce, "Hey, they're *fightin'*!"

Without a word I strode out of the cabin, down the porch steps and around the side toward the two figures pummeling and grunting on the ground just at the edge of the woods. As I approached them, I saw Mack standing near his cabin watching with a smile on his face. I reached down and pulled up the two cursing assailants.

"We're supposed to be working," I said patiently. "Let's go."

"Well, he ain't workin'!" Marty Gingold flared, his usually slicked-down hair ruffled and dusty.

Tony said nothing. He just stared at Marty with dead, hating eyes.

"What do you mean, he's not working?" I asked.

"He's just sittin' on his ass on a rock. Well, if ya think I'm workin' when *he* don't, you're full of o'—"

"All right, all right," I interrupted. "Go on. Police. I'll talk to Tony."

Marty brushed himself off as he waddled away, muttering something about wops.

"Fat-ass *kike*!" Tony yelled after him, teeth clenched.

Marty whirled, fists suddenly clenched but I waved him off. "Go on," I said. "Go on."

Marty cursed to himself as he went off. He kicked a rock across the uneven ground. "Teacher's pet," he said. Tony lunged forward but I caught him by the arm and jerked him back.

I led him into the woods and sat him down on a log.

"Well, what is it now?" I asked.

He pressed his thin lips together and said nothing.

"Tony, we have work to do. *All* of us."

"Fuck it," he muttered.

I blew out a heavy breath.

"Tony, are we going to part friends or not?"

"Who gives a—"

"*Tony.*"

He looked up at me, the skin drawing tautly over the bones in his thin face.

"What do I give a fuck for this camp!" he said furiously. "Ya can shove it up ya—"

"That's *enough*!" I wanted to drag him up by the arm and make him work. But I didn't. I looked at him a moment longer, then said, "All right. Forget it. You don't have to do anything. Just sit here all day long and *stew*. It'll give you a fine memory of your last day at Camp Pleasant."

"What do *I* care?"

"You care," I said. "More than any of them."

I turned and went back to the cabin where Chester had just spilled his pail of water for the third time. He began giggling hysterically as an outraged Charlie Barnett kicked over his pail and stomped in the puddles of water.

With my help, they finally finished up the floor, before it became waterlogged. Then we went out to do the screens. Marty Gingold was talking to the Moody boys.

"All done policing?" I asked him.

"Why should *I* police?" he asked bitterly. "Rocca ain't."

"Listen," I said. "You don't know a thing about Rocca. But remember this: He's had one hell of a life. A life so hard that none of you can even imagine how bad it was. That's all I can tell you about that but remember that the camp's closing is hitting him hard. I know, I know," I said, cutting off Marty's protestations, "it's hitting you hard too. Well, it's not the same, believe me. You're going back to a nice home, to people who love you. He isn't. Now will you stop being so damn petty and forget about him. You'll never even *see* him after tomorrow."

"That's not too soon for *me*," said Marty Gingold.

"Yeah," I said. "Sure. Come on. Each of you take a screen. Let's get them cleaned."

This took about an hour, what with releasing the rust-stuck catches, lugging the screens up to Paradise where the hoses were, waiting our turn, then returning to the cabin with the washed screens and reinstalling them. At eleven-thirty came swimming time. The dock buzzer sounded and the sweaty boys rushed down the hill to splash in the lake.

Tony and I were alone in the cabin. He half-lay, half-sat on his bunk staring at a comic book. I could hear his heavy breathing in the silence as I lay there staring at the overhead bunk.

"Why *should* we leave?" he suddenly said.

I lifted my head a little and looked over at his hard, resentful face.

"You know exactly why," I said.

"Just because the fat guy's dead?"

"Forget it," I said, turning on my side.

He cursed to himself.

"If you want to curse, get out of here," I said.

I heard him fling his comic book on the floor. Then his sneakers hit the floor and I heard the scrape of his baseball bat as he dragged it away from its leaning place against the wall.

"Ain't *none* o' ya care!" he said, and his toughness cracked right down the middle for a moment. "None o' ya care about nothin'!"

The screen door slapped shut behind him and I heard his footsteps as he moved away. I shouldn't have done that, I thought. He was hurting enough. I lay there staring at the wall, feeling my heart thud slowly in my chest like the fist of a dying man on the wall of his prison.

Lunchtime; a rehash of breakfast. After it was over, our cabin stayed in the dining hall and, with the aid of Mack's cabin, scrubbed the floor. I looked through the *Lost and Found* box and found three of Tony's tee-shirts, one of his sport shirts, two of his towels and his rain hat. I sent him back to the cabin with them.

As the afternoon progressed, I kept getting more and more tense, thinking about Merv. What if he hadn't done it? Then there could be no hope at all. I went to the office to see Sid.

"Is he back yet?" I asked.

He shook his head. "Not till five or after, Matt," he said. Doc was in Emmetsville to see Ellen and find out about Merv.

"Oh. All right."

"Matt, you're not getting up too much hope on this?"

I swallowed. "I was the one who didn't think we should even *tell* the sheriff about it, remember?"

"I know that," he said. "But you want to believe it. Don't you?"

"Don't *you?*"

"Sure I do," he said. "But I'm not going to until we know for sure."

"All right." I left the office without another word.

Time passing. Minutes spinning past, hours ticking by. The last day of camp. Merv in town being questioned. Ellen waiting to know if she was innocent or not. All of us in camp waiting, waiting. The last day of camp.

The four-thirty buzzer went off. The boys raced for their bathing suits while Mack and I finished pushing the tables back into place.

"Don't hurt your wrist," I told him.

"It's okay," he said in the tone of voice which indicated nothing of his feelings.

When I left the dining hall, Mack walked beside me. I didn't know why but I held back a little so as not to move ahead. Our relationship since the fight and, especially, since Ed's death had been virtually non-existent. We nodded to one another in passing but that was about the extent of it. I had no idea how he felt toward me.

"Well," he said, as we started across the bridge, "I guess this winds it up."

"Guess," I said. "A pity too. Most of these kids want to stay."

He nodded. "'Specially that little wop of yours," he said.

I forced down the tightening. He'd used the term without guile. I realized abruptly that he was one of those who could call a colored man a nigger without realizing it was an insult.

"I suppose so," I said.

"Sid told me about him," Mack said. "I didn't know before."

I nodded. "Uh-huh."

"You comin' back next year?" he asked.

I glanced over to see if he was smiling. But there wasn't a trace of mockery on his face and there hadn't been any in his voice.

"I doubt it," I said.

He nodded once. "Well," he said, "I...hope ya don't hold no grudge against me."

I stared at him. "I—"

"Take it easy, Matt," he said, heading for his cabin.

I watched him until he'd gone in. Then, almost dazedly, I went into my cabin. We'd been enemies. I'd hated his guts, he'd hated mine; we'd fought. Now this.

It's guys like Arthur MacNeil that make life confusing.

✳ ✳ ✳

Doc returned near the end of supper. I saw the truck pull in off the road and, through the screen door, I watched him walk slowly toward the office.

I couldn't eat. I tried to wait a while and not rush in on him. But I couldn't hold myself. After a few minutes of rising tension, I got up and crossed the floor quickly, my legs feeling numb, my heart beating in slow, gigantic thuds.

He was sitting slumped at his desk, staring at the blotter. When the door shut behind me, he turned and looked at me without a word. He didn't even have to say it.

"*Why?*" I asked, not even conscious of the frail shaking sound my voice was.

"His friend says they were eating breakfast when it happened," Doc told me. He shook his head once, eyes lowering. "There's no evidence, son. The sheriff had to let him go."

"Oh...*Christ*." I put my left hand over my eyes and sank down on a chair. I hadn't realized it till then but I was staking everything on Merv's being guilty. It was the one prop I had left. Now it was kicked out from under me and I was falling.

3.

At eight o'clock that night the entire camp assembled in the Fire Circle, which was a rough circle of log benches arranged in tiers around a smaller brick circle in which the fires were lit.

It was just beginning to get dark. The bonfire crackled loudly, its fluttering orange-yellow arms reaching high above the logs, filling the air with darting sparks which disappeared like short-lived fireflies. I remember that scene vividly—night edging in around us until only the fire kept it out. All of us sitting in that blackness, boys and counselors all huddled together in a circle of glowing, fiery light.

Doc said a few words, so did Sid and Jack and Barney. It's been a nice summer, we're glad you came, sorry it had to end this way. We sang a few songs. I directed, watching the faces of the boys flicker with the light and shadow; hearing the sputtering crackle of the fire behind me, feeling its buffeting head; hearing the joined voices sing as only boys can sing when they're around a campfire and feeling different.

"Should aulde acquaintance be forgot and the days of aulde lang syne."

When the meeting was over, flashlights were unsheathed and the night was flayed open by slashing white beams. The dark paths became passages of criss-crossed white ribbons dancing up and down and sideways as, talking in mysterious night voices, the boys returned to the cabins for their last night's sleep in Camp Pleasant.

The overhead bulb of Cabin Thirteen seemed particularly bare and sterile after the warm glow of the fire. It ended the momentary feeling of nostalgia the singing had brought about and seemed to point up the harshness of farewell.

It being the last night, Charlie Barnett and Marty Gingold decided a general roughhouse was in order. To this Chester and the Moody boys were more than amicable. I didn't stop them since all the cabins were exploding at the seams. I left the cabin when the horseplay started and headed for Paradise with my toothbrush and paste.

Paradise had a few customers in it preparing for bed; the boys who, one day, would doubtlessly brush their teeth under enemy fire, the oblivious neat who move concisely through life, unruffled and dispassionate.

When I returned to the cabin, I found my mattress and bedclothes lying across one of the rafters and a mottle-faced Jim Moody yelling for succor where he'd been bound to the center post of the cabin. From the trembling conspirators under their blankets came ill-muffled giggles.

I released Jim Moody who pounced on his brother with a vengeful curse. I ignored the battle while I replaced my mattress and made up the bunk.

Then I made the rolling Moodys get in bed and checked each undercover man. Tony was the only one not there. I put Chester in charge of the cabin and told him his head would roll if there were any more disturbances before I came back. Then I turned out the light and went looking for Tony. All along the rows of cabins, lights were going out and imperfect stillness settling.

I walked around the Senior Division a while but Tony wasn't there. I went down the hill and looked in the dark lodge but he wasn't there. I looked on the dock and in the dining hall but he wasn't there either.

On the verge of getting alarmed, I found him sitting on the visiting team bench of the ball field. He was leaning on his *Louisville Slugger* as an old man sitting on a sunlit bench will lean upon his cane.

"Bedtime, Tony," I said.

He didn't speak or budge. He kept staring out at the moon-gleaming diamond with listless eyes.

"Come on, Tony."

"Yeah." He sighed heavily and got up without another word.

We started back to the cabin. I tried to put my arm around his shoulders but he twisted away and I let my arm drop, feeling as if he were a tightly wound spring ready to leap at the slightest touch.

Back in the cabin, I waited while he got out of his clothes and slipped between his grimy sheets.

"All packed?" I asked, and he shrugged carelessly. I checked his foot locker and found his clothes all there—what was left of them anyway. It looked like a pile of soiled laundry. Closing the top of the locker, I straightened up and flicked off the light.

"Goodnight, Tony," I said. He didn't answer.

Silence in my cabin. I lay on the bunk staring up at the overhead mattress sagging with the not inconsequential weight of Chester Wickerly. I tried to think about them all going home tomorrow—Chester, Charlie, Marty, the Moody brothers. I tried to think about David and his mother. I tried to concentrate on Tony and his problems; but all I could think about was Ellen.

I don't know when I fell asleep; the transition between consciousness and unconsciousness was too subtle to be noticed. I remember dreaming though. Ellen and I were in a long, dark hallway and there were black figures coming toward us from both directions. Ellen clung to me, terrified. I remember how she clutched at my arm. The black figures had flashlights and they kept shining them into our eyes. Ellen began to scream. She was screaming and screaming and—

Screaming!

I jolted up in bed with a gasp, my head snapping around.

Tony was screaming as if he'd lost his mind. His screams rang out shrilly in the dark cabin, pouring endlessly from his throat. I heard one of the boys call out, "Jesus, what's *wrong*!"

Heart pounding, I flung off the blankets and jumped over to Tony's bunk. I saw the dark outline of him sitting bolt upright in his bunk, screaming.

"Tony!" I said.

He kept screaming.

"*Tony*!" I sat down quickly beside him and grabbed his arms.

"No!" he cried in a horror-stricken voice.

I grabbed his shoulders and shook him as he screamed again in my face.

"Tony, wake up!"

The light flashed on and, glancing aside, I saw Marty Gingold standing by the switch in his pajamas, mouth and eyes round with shock.

"What's up?" he asked breathlessly.

"Turn it out!" I ordered.

The cabin was plunged into darkness again and I turned back to Tony who was sobbing now, trying to talk in a guttural, jerky voice.

"Didn't," he gasped, "I tell ya I *didn't*. Le' me alone, ya bastid, le' me alone!"

"Tony, be quiet."

"I didn't," he sobbed, "I didn't do nothin'. It ain't m-my fault. It ain't. I didn't—"

I clapped my hand over his mouth, suddenly understanding. I don't know why I knew; I just did. It came as more of a physical reaction than anything. A prickling sensation along my spine, a sudden numbing of my hands and feet.

He began struggling wildly in my grip. I felt his teeth dig into my hand and, with a dull cry, I jerked it away.

"Le' me alone!" he screamed. "You're dead! You're *dead*!"

I clapped my hand over his mouth again, glancing aside in panic as the light in Mack's cabin came on. I pushed Tony back on the pillow, feeling the pounding rush of blood in my temples and wrists.

"What's wrong?" I heard Mack call out.

"Nothin'!" I yelled back. "A bad dream."

"Oh."

I bent over Tony and put my lips close to his ear as he writhed insanely in my grip.

"Tony, it's Matt, it's Matt," I whispered, hardly able to breathe. "It's all right, Tony, all right. Go to sleep. Go to sleep, baby, it's all right. It's all right, Tony, it's all *right*." I felt hot tears running down my cheeks. "It's all right, Tony," I whispered, "It's all right."

"What'sa matter?" demanded Charlie Barnett.

"Go to sleep, it's all right," I said. "Just a bad dream."

Then I turned back to Tony and sat there staring through my tears at the little boy who had killed Ed Nolan. I sat there stroking his hair with fingers I could barely feel. Tony, Tony; his name kept repeating itself in my mind. I couldn't say another word to him.

After a while he fell asleep but I still sat there, looking down at his face. Even though I couldn't see it, I could imagine it—thin, tear-streaked, those dark circles under his swollen eyes, those little pinched, worry lines that scarred his face even when he slept.

I don't know how long I sat there. I felt like a block of stone. Odd, I kept thinking, ever since it happened, I'd felt as if I'd give half my life to know that Ellen was innocent. Now I knew it and it had only plunged me deeper into despair.

After a time, I stood up, feeling as if my legs were running into the floor boards. Slowly, with the motions of a drugged man, I put on my bathrobe and slippers and closed the screen door silently behind me.

It was a beautiful night. The sky was ebony black and cloudless, dotted with sprinkles of bright stars and with a great white saucer of a moon. Dark trees rustled in the cool wind and the air was filled with the peaceful sounds of night. I stumbled along, not noticing at all. I crossed the bridge and heard the stream gurgling underneath as it flowed down to the dark lake. I walked past the stillness of the dining hall and down the path past the leader's tent.

There was a light burning in Doc's tent. I found him slumped over his table, his head on his arms. I stood in the tent entrance a little while looking at him, watching his gray hair ruffle slightly in the breeze. I even wondered if I should go back to my cabin and forget about it.

Then, with a sigh, I spoke his name. He didn't move. I stepped over to him and touched his shoulder. He grunted and raised his head, then blinked and stared at me for a moment before recognition came.

"Son?" he asked then in a dull, sleep-ridden voice.

I stared at him without speaking.

"What is it, son?" he asked, standing up.

My bathrobe rustled as I sank down on his cot.

"Tony did it," I said. It was like driving a knife into myself.

I wasn't prepared for the look of complete blankness on his face. I'd expected him to gasp, maybe even recoil with shock. He just sat down slowly, looking at me as if he hadn't even heard what I said. Then, in the stillness, I heard him swallow dryly. His eyes fell and he drew in a long breath.

"So you know," he murmured.

I felt the skin tightening across my face. "What do you—?" I started.

"I've known it all along," he said. "The day it happened—I saw him come running out of the Nolan cabin. I didn't know what had—happened. I just thought he'd gone to—I don't know what I thought. I meant to speak to him about it later. Then you found Ed."

I felt as if my breath had stopped.

"You let Ellen go to jail?" I asked incredulously. "You—"

I stopped as our eyes met.

"What would you have done?" he asked quietly. "You come to me now, not knowing what to do."

He shook his head.

"I feel exactly as you do, son," he said. "A complete—*disbelief.* It can't be real, it must be a dream. A boy. *A ten-year-old boy.* What would they do to him? Execute him? No. But...maybe that would be even kinder than—"

He shook his head again and let out his breath slowly.

We sat looking at each other in the dim light, and I knew exactly why he hadn't spoken of it. I was in love with Ellen but, even to me, the thought of turning in Tony seemed hideous. I knew why Doc had looked so worn and unhappy all the past weeks. It must have been a terrible weight to bear alone.

"I thought it might not be necessary to mention it," he said. "There's so little real evidence. I thought maybe no one would be held. But...."

I looked at him.

"Her lawyer told me there's no hope of an acquittal," he said. "There's no evidence working for her."

He was quiet. I sat looking at him, feeling torn in two.

"Doc, we've got to!" I burst out suddenly.

He raised his eyes.

"It sounds simple," he said. "Just tell the sheriff that ten-year-old Tony Rocca killed his camp director."

"But if we testified," I said, "Tony was driven to it, you know that. If we told what happened."

"He'd still be put away, son," Doc said. "No matter how lenient they are, no matter how much they consider his situation—they'll be forced to put him away again." He shook his head miserably. "How could he survive it? How?"

We sat there silently, looking at the wooden floor. I kept thinking of Tony. Of how he must have thought with his boy-like logic that killing Ed was the answer. He'd get back in his own cabin then and everything would be all right. All he had to do was get rid of "the fat guy."

I visualized him finding the hunting knife, maybe in the *Lost and Found* box, maybe he stole it. I saw him going down to the Nolan cabin without a plan, without any more precaution than going there when the rest of the camp was on the dock for the diving show. Or maybe there *had* been a plan, maybe there was a core of terrible shrewdness in him that his past life had caused.

But the rest was accident; Ellen being unconscious in the bathroom, Ed asleep on the living-room couch. Tony stealing in, the knife in his bandaged hand, that taut, wild look on his face.

"Jesus Christ," I said, "what did they *do* to the poor kid?"

Doc murmured, "Yes. What did they do?"

4.

When I woke up in the morning, the first thing I tried to do was believe it had all been a dream. For a long minute, lying there on my side and staring at the latticework of sunlight on the cabin wall, I almost managed to believe it; it was so completely far-fetched and bizarre.

Then I raised up on one elbow and saw Tony lying on his stomach, looking at me. He turned quickly onto his back with a rustle of bedclothes and I felt those cold fingers clamp shut on my insides again. It was true.

A wave of sickening despair fell across me as I looked at him. *Ten years old*, I thought. I remembered the first day I'd met him. I remembered his tense, angry pride, how he'd chosen to risk drowning rather than admit he couldn't swim. I thought of how he'd remained silent about his torn foot because he was afraid to tell anyone. I thought of his lying about his mother's letter, thought about that little song he sang. I thought about his endless truculent and yet pathetic search for happiness. He'd wanted only to be a boy but the world had not allowed it. It had driven him from youth.

"I s'pose ya'll tell the cops," Tony said.

I twitched in surprise and stared at him, unable to speak.

"Who cares?" he said, struggling to sound unconcerned. "It don't matter t'me."

"Oh...*Tony*."

Reveille then; Willie Pratt's last assault upon our ears. There was a rush of activity up the cabin line. This was not a day to stay in bed. My boys all dressed quickly, several of them staring guardedly at Tony. While he was lacing his sneakers, Chester whispered to me, "What'd he mean about cops?"

I shook my head. "Nothing."

He didn't look convinced and, when he and Jim Moody left for Paradise, I saw them talking in confederate tones.

Tony had managed to force a mantle of casualness upon himself. He kept whistling between his teeth while he dressed, packed the last of his clothes and rolled up his mattress to be carried down to the lodge later. Only the constant, erratic jerking of his chest as he breathed gave him away; that and his voice which was strained and brittle.

174

"*No more camp*," he said. "Ain't that a damn shame?"

No one spoke. Whistling louder yet, Tony left the cabin and headed for Paradise.

Charlie and Marty were at me. "What was he yellin' for last night?" Marty probed. "What was he talkin' about?"

"Nothing," I said. "I *told* you—he had a bad dream."

"Ye-ah?" asked a suspicious Charlie Barnett.

"*Yeah*. Now get ready for breakfast." There was a sinking sensation in my stomach as if someone were piling cold stones there.

I didn't go to Paradise because I didn't want to see Tony. I combed my hair and went to the dining hall kitchen and threw some water in my face, drying it with a handkerchief. When I came out of the kitchen, Sid was heading for the Senior cabins. He saw me and came over.

"I was just coming to see you," he said and, from the way he said it, I knew that Doc had told him.

"Have you told anyone else yet?" he asked.

I shook my head. "Just Doc."

He nodded. "Well," he said, "Doc still isn't sure." He paused a moment, then said, "But I am. We'll wait a while and see what happens."

"Then what?" I asked.

"I'll call the sheriff," he said quietly. "We can't let Ellen be sacrificed—no matter what it means to Tony."

I didn't nod or shake my head or speak or do anything. Sid put his hand on my arm and tightened the fingers.

"I feel as rotten as you do about this, Matt," he said. "But it's out of our hands. We have no right to even think about sacrificing one human being for another. It's not our privilege."

"No," I said, hardly audible. I stood there watching him as he walked back toward the office.

175

Breakfast. All of us sitting around the table, not talking much, drinking our orange juice. I noticed Charlie and Marty exchange a meaningful glance, then Charlie seemed to brace himself. He drew in a quick breath and blurted it out suddenly without warning.

"Ya know what Tony told us?" he asked.

My hand twitched involuntarily and drops of orange juice dashed across the table. I glanced at Tony and saw him staring at Charlie, his nostrils flared a little, his chest rising and falling slowly and heavily, a crazy little smile pulling up his lips.

"Eat your breakfast," I said in a husky voice.

"But d'ya know what he told us?" Marty insisted.

"I don't *care* what he told you!" I snapped. "It's not my business." I felt as if they were closing in on me; as if I had to stop them before it was too late.

"Yeah, but—" Charlie and Marty started, almost simultaneously.

"But *nothing!*" I cut it short. "Eat your breakfast I said."

They all looked at each other, exchanging wary, suspicious glances. The juice seemed to turn to acid in my stomach. It was like a disease, this information. It seemed to be spreading. In a second now, someone at the next table would acquire it—Mack, maybe one of his boys. Then on to the next table—the next—a hideous wildfire of knowledge.

"I told 'em—"

"Tony, *shut up!*" I said furiously, feeling my stomach muscles go rigid. I don't know what I had in mind. I knew it had to come out and yet I couldn't bear the thought.

"He said he killed Big Ed," Charlie Barnett finished it.

It was as if we'd all turned to stone. We sat there without moving or speaking, staring at each other and that smile was frozen to Tony's tense, white face. I tried to think of something to say, something that would end this moment, dispel it—but I couldn't. It was Tony who ended it.

"That's right," he said casually, as if he were admitting the theft of a candy bar.

The boys were almost as speechless as I was in the face of such a revelation.

"He's kiddin' us, ain't he?" Jim Moody finally said in a frail voice.

"Hell, I'm kiddin'!" Tony said defiantly. "I stuck a—"

"*Tony!*"

I hadn't meant to be so loud but they heard me at the next table and turned to see what was the matter.

"I'll tell if I want!" Tony yelled back, the skin like drum-hide across his cheeks, an unnoticed tear lacing suddenly across his face.

"Tony, will you stop?" My voice was strengthless now. I was pleading with him.

He sank back against his chair, that smile flickering on his lips, breath failing him.

"I did it," he said, as if it were a compulsive need for him to say it. "I killed the fat guy. None o' you dopes had the nerve. Well, I did. *I did.*"

I stood up on trembling legs and put my hand on Tony's shoulder.

"Come on," I said in a hollow voice.

"We goin' t'town?" he asked, still trying to sound confident but unable to.

"Yes," I said. From the corners of my eyes, I saw the boys staring at him with faces shocked into immobile masks.

I'll remember that walk until I die. It wasn't far—just to the office—but it seemed as if everyone in the dining hall were watching. It seemed to grow quiet as Tony and I walked across the floor. I felt eyes on us.

Then I saw Doc and Sid rising, looking stunned, and I opened the office door and ushered Tony in.

When Doc and Sid came in, Tony was sitting down on a chair against the wall, looking at a map as if he were interested in it.

"What is it?" Doc asked quickly.

"He's told the boys," I said. "It'll be all over the camp before the buses come. It's no use trying to keep it secret any more. It's...no use waiting." I almost whispered the words.

We stood there looking down wordlessly at Tony. After a long moment, he turned around and looked up at us, his thin face blank.

Tony Rocca grinned at us.

"Hi," he said.

5.

Ellen and I sat quietly in the taxicab as it drove along the lakeside road, heading for Camp Pleasant. We hadn't said a word since leaving Emmetsville almost an hour before. We just sat there, her hand in mine, staring ahead. Our bodies shifted a little as the taxi turned right at the crossroads and I felt her press against me. I turned to her and tried to smile. Our eyes held for a moment and then she turned her head away.

"I—almost wish you hadn't found out," she said quietly. "I believed I did it. I was almost resigned."

I shook my head. "That wouldn't have helped him," I said. "It wouldn't have—saved him."

We were still again.

When we reached the camp, I told the driver to wait for us and we entered the camp grounds. We stood in the open area in front of the dining hall and there wasn't a sound except for the rustling of the trees.

"So quiet," I said. "I can't ever remember it being this quiet in the daytime."

She said nothing.

"Well," I said. We started for the cabin.

As we moved, I saw her lips press together into a tight line.

"It's all right," I said. "I'm with you."

She smiled but it wasn't a reassured smile.

We met Sid on the path. He smiled warmly as he came up to us.

"Ellen," he said, "it's good to see you again. How are you?"

"I'm fine, Sid. Thank you," she said.

"Good." He looked at me. "Hello, Matt," he said.

"Hi."

There was a pause.

"Well," Sid said then, "she's all wrapped up for the winter."

"My cabin all right?" I asked.

"Yeah, Mack nailed it up for you."

"Oh. Everybody's gone then?"

"Everybody." He nodded. "I'm the only one left and I'm going now." He smiled at Ellen. "I'm very happy you're free," he said. "What are you planning to do now?"

She swallowed nervously. "I don't know exactly, Sid," she said.

"We're staying in Emmetsville until Tony's case is decided," I said.

"Oh?" Sid smiled politely. "I see." I noticed the strained smile on Ellen's face.

"Well," Sid said, "I guess I'll lock up the office and take off then. You'll lock up the cabin?"

"We will," I said, shaking his hand.

"Fine. Think you'll be back next year?" he asked.

"I don't think so, Sid," I said. "I've...I don't think so."

He nodded, smiling. "Well, if you do," he said, "I'll be here. So long. Good luck. To both of you."

We watched him walking away. "He's a good man," I said.

"Yes. He is," she said.

The cabin was very still as we approached it. Ellen hesitated.

"Come on," I said. "It's just an empty cabin."

"I wish it were," she murmured, and I knew what she meant.

We went in and stood a moment in the cool, shadowy kitchen.

"This is where we met," I said.

"Yes."

She stopped in the living-room doorway and looked in with pained eyes.

"That bad?" I asked.

She let out a restless breath. "It's bad," she said.

"Would you rather wait outside while I pack your things?" I asked.

"No," she said. "No, I—" She broke off and looked at me without meeting my eyes. "Shall we talk about it?" she asked.

"About what?"

She moved over to a chair and let herself down, her eyes avoiding the sight of the couch. I saw her chest tremble with breath, then she clasped her hands and got control of herself.

"Sit down, Matt," she said.

I started for her. "No, the couch," she said. I looked surprised. "Please," she said.

I sat down on the couch, glancing down involuntarily and seeing, with relief, that everything had been cleaned up.

"What is it, Ellen?"

She looked at her tightly clasped hands.

"What are *you* planning to do, Matt?" she asked.

I looked at her a moment. Then I said, "First I want to stay with Tony. Help him all I can."

She nodded.

"Of course," she said.

"Then I want to work with boys," I went on, putting it into words at last. "I mean the rest of my life. All this summer I've...sort of had a feeling about it. A feeling about boys; how so many of them need help, guidance. It's what I want to do, Ellen. I've decided that definitely. Maybe Tony decided it for me. Anyway, it's a path I've always looked for; the direction I need. I guess working at Camp Pleasant sort of...*crystallized* my whole life." I looked at her carefully. "In many ways," I said. Later I'd tell her about Julia. When she was ready.

All through my speech she sat there, expressionless, listening. When I was through, she nodded again.

"I think that's very wonderful," she said, but she sounded withdrawn and unhappy about it.

"But it's not a work to be done alone," I said.

Her eyes lifted to mine suddenly.

"Matt," she said, "I'm only going to ask you one question." Her eyes dropped to her hands again. "*Are you sure?*" she asked.

"About working with—?"

"Matt, you *know* I don't mean that!" She sounded close to tears.

It hit me suddenly. I got up and went toward her.

"Matt, don't. *Please*," she begged. "It only makes it harder to—"

But I went on my knees before her, her shaking hands in mine.

"Matt, it's different now," she said. "You *know* it's different. Before, you felt pity for me, you were—"

I put my hand across her mouth and her eyes were like the eyes of a stricken deer—gentle and frightened.

"Ellen, when will you learn?" I asked quietly. "When will you *learn?*"

I drew away my fingers. "I love you," I said. "This work I'm talking about: Do you think it would mean anything to me *alone?* Ellen, I couldn't do it alone. I need you to help me."

There was a glistening in her eyes.

"It's what you want?" she whispered hesitantly. "It's what yo*u—really* want?"

I put my hands on her warm cheeks. "It's what I want," I said gently.

Her lips under mine were warm and yielding and, beneath my touch, I could almost feel the long-extinguished fires in her starting to burn again.

We packed her things quickly—her clothes, her records, her few books; those few items which were the only things left to remind her of her marriage to a man who might already have been dead a hundred years.

Then we locked the cabin behind us. But, before we started back for the taxi, I took her in my arms and kissed her for a long time. When it was over, she said nothing; she didn't have to—her eyes said it for her. We picked up her suitcases and moved along the path, past the leader's tent, past the locked dispensary, across the great open area in front of the silent dining hall and into the taxicab.

Our hands clasped tightly as we drove away from Camp Pleasant. And we never went back. We never wanted to go back.